P9-BJR-450

YOUR EMOTICONS WON'T SAVE YOU

for the real Alex

For Elizabeth,   2/2013

♡ ;)
YOUR EMOTICONS WON'T SAVE YOU

a novella and poems

ETHAN NICHTERN

All best and see you
soon on the road

-ethan

"What my eyes saw was simultaneous; what I shall transcribe is successive, because language is successive."
Jorge Luis Borges, *The Aleph*

"Emoticons...can change and improve the interpretation of plain text."
Wikipedia

CAMP, HAPPY, AND THE
SLIGHTLY IMPERFECT WIFEBEATERS
;)

THE METRO-NORTH

"WE'RE GOIN' TO CAMP!" GIDEON SHOUTS IN my ear, channeling his six-year-old self as he drags his heavy suitcase toward the station's central kiosk. Feeling dizzy, I barely keep pace, wondering what it would feel like to actually throw up in Grand Central's crowded terminal, to juxtapose the chaos in my gut onto the remodeled elegance of this floor. Anthony is standing beneath a polished clock with his gear, shaking his head at us. "Two minutes," is all he says as he hands us each a one-way ticket. He starts jogging athletically, jetting and weaving impossibly fast through the throngs toward Track 20. Somehow, Gideon and I keep him in sight, his shiny REI camping pack bobbing among Saturday travelers.

On the ramp to the platform, I lean over for a moment and drop my duffel. This time, I'm sure I'm actually gonna vomit. I feel that sinking feeling you get with involuntary bodily processes, when a "maybe" is about to become a "just-did." But this wave passes like the last one. I follow Gideon and Anthony onto the train just before the departure bell rings.

Inside the car, I lean my throbbing head against the sliding doors, trying to reconstruct what happened in the last 18 hours. There's a random image of the first girl who ever unzipped my pants, but I have no idea where it came from. I haven't seen her in over two years. Then I think of my best girl friend Amelia's face in the fluorescent Brooklyn diner after dusk, and everything comes back to me. Amelia and I spent all of yesterday afternoon together, searching our high school neighborhood of Brooklyn

Heights for scenes for her to photograph. We ended up at a diner in downtown Brooklyn where we each ordered a milkshake, hers chocolate and mine strawberry, talking about old school things in our old school neighborhood.

"Everyone I've seen this summer used to be so much...happier," she said, as I slurped the last slurpable bit of foam through the straw.

"I mean..." I answered, feeling a little defensive on behalf of everyone, "that's 'cause we went to a Quaker School. Everyone was also bored outta their minds."

Under the diner's harsh light, Amelia shook her head hard in disagreement. "Every picture I have of you from high school, Alex, you're smiling like *crazy.*" She looked like she was about to say something else about me, something *trés* annoying about who I am and who I used to be and who I should become, but she didn't. That's when my bad mood came on. Then she started talking about the three kids from our tiny graduating class who'd spent time in mental institutions this year—including the first girl who'd ever unzipped my pants, which was news to me—and my mood got worse. Then Amelia's boyfriend showed up and hijacked the entire conversation, and I felt miserable. I bounced back to Manhattan and found Gideon, my-old-friend-made-new-again by the summer's escapades, at a bar near his parents' apartment on Washington Square.

That's right about when last night came undone. Gideon has a miraculous rapport with bartenders (of both genders) that benefits everyone, and he's got so much unstoppable energy in his drunken voice that you'd think consequence is just a fairy tale. We got real drunk. We figured we could just sleep it off in the car today. Neither one of us can be asked to drive, license-less, unless we want to roll like derelicts up the Northeast corridor. Lucas won't let us get anywhere near the wheel of his Range Rover anyway, and Gabe, who just got his license last week himself, is extra nervous about anyone driving his parents' car.

What can I say, I failed my drivers' test after taking driver's ed. senior year in high school. I took the test the day after Grandma died, way up in the Bronx for some reason, and I couldn't focus on the road or three-point turns. I didn't take the test again. What's the point? I'm a New Yorker, where a car chains you down, and when I'm in the City I'm just visiting, and when I'm up at school I'm just visiting, and when I go to Europe I'll be just visiting too.

The Bonanza Bus to Port Authority is pretty cheap, so that's how I roll for the most part during the school year, throwing down my father's credit card before the foggy plexiglass counter and signing the male signature I haven't developed into my own. I just write Alexander Bardo in the same messy script, which I guess makes it mine regardless. Then I get on the bus and watch Rhode Island turn into Connecticut turn into Westchester turn into the general radius of home.

But most visits this past school year, despite the familiar jagged outlines, the City didn't feel like home. Grandma was gone—the kind of gone that isn't vague anymore—and most streets were covered with the mist of her absence. Usually I made it worse by coming home spontaneously, without coordinating with my two remaining high school friends. And when I went on long solitary walks or chilled alone on my father's roof—telling myself out loud all the things I wanted to say to the world, things that seemed crucially insightful in my mind and then unimpressive as soon as their sentence finished— the City felt like a foggy hologram. And when that feeling hit, I couldn't get Sophie out of my mind, like the lyrics to a song you aren't even sure you like anymore. Sophie was even more gone than Grandma, which is ironic, because Sophie's still alive.

This summer has been different though. I reunited with my boys from camp—and there was a party almost every night on Gideon's warm balcony overlooking Washington Square. The metropolis beyond the balcony felt like crystal and concrete again, inhabited by people, not ghosts.

◆

The Metro-North train is ridiculously crowded. Anthony's still pissed. He's got that look on him that says we are amateurs when it comes to motion, that Anthony is the real deal Traveling Man, the only one who really knows what he is doing. And he does: he bought tickets for us in advance, knowing we'd be cutting it close.

His eyes float over the packed car, finding no seats anywhere. "That's fuckin' great, guys."

"The subway took forever," I half-apologize. My eyes are closed and my head swims, skull leaning heavily against the glass as the car door closes behind me. "Yeah, well I took the same fuckin' subway," Anthony says.

"Ours took longer. We probably just missed the one you got on."

"Ant, could you chill, please?" Gideon adds. "I have to drag this big-ass suitcase." In 10 minutes, he'd thrown all the semester's essentials from his parents' apartment into one huge bag. The suitcase sags behind him on its overstressed wheels. My backpack and a small duffel are strapped to my shoulders, three days worth of clothes for a six-day trip, because I didn't do laundry recently. Anthony—aka Mr Lonely Planet, Traveling Man—has his obnoxiously professional camping pack and matching duffel. I look at my watch. It's 10:41 am, Saturday, August 22, 1998, and we're underground, tunneling northward.

"What'd you kids do last night?" Anthony asks, his face finally lightening.

"We just chilled for awhile at that bar," Gideon says. It got kinda dead eventually. I kicked it to another fat chick."

"Hey, what else is new?" Anthony chuckles. We rise above ground around 100th street and pass uptown, through Harlem, over the metallic bridge into the South Bronx and then northward, out of the city, into Westchester. Our crowded car empties at Rye.

"What the hell is so important in Rye?" Anthony asks.

"Rye Playland," I answer.

"We're going to our own *Playland*," Anthony says without missing a beat, and chuckles again. We shuffle into the conjoined group of four seats by us—Anthony and I facing forward, Gideon facing backward across from me, my knees touching his. Anthony made sandwiches for all of us and brought apples, lots of apples. He's communal like that; he really is an expert on socialized motion. I thank him through my headache and try to pry a smile from his face. He hands me a bundle of plastic wrap.

"Want an apple?" he asks earnestly. I put the sandwich in my backpack for later and take the fruit. It's the best kind—the smallish kind that swirl red and green, Technicolor yin and yang. The withered leaf still clings gingerly to the stem. I have no idea what it's called, but it's by far the best apple. I take a tiny bite. The apple is crisp, and I'm a little more at peace with my hangover.

We get out in Greenwich, CT. Sometimes I think about staying on a train past my stop, but the ticket guy already swiped the stubs from overhead. No one with somewhere to be wants to stay on past their stop, anyway. No one wants to feel like they're getting kicked out though, either. The feeling that I *have* to leave a train makes me feel even more homeless than the feeling of being stuck on a train. We can't see Lucas' Range Rover anywhere, or Lucas or Gabe. We assume they're late, but as I walked to the pay phone I hear Lucas' loud and cracking voice call out "Alex." He and Gabe are parked past the swarms of people, the gleaming Rover and Gabe's parents' dusty Mazda side by side. We grab hands and exchange hugs.

"You kids ready to go?" Lucas asks, excited.

"We're goin' to camp!" Gideon yells again. Everyone laughs at his exuberance. Sometimes, when he isn't flirting with every sentient being with a cervix in a 100-yard radius, Gideon really does sound like a six-year-old. He's the only one of us who didn't go to Lucas' father's camp back in the day, and the person who has the least reason to take a road trip now, except that he gets a free ride to school. That'll be the last stop. We're gonna head up to Camp Winnisquam in New Hampshire for some playtime, then head to Ithaca to drop Gideon off and chill for another few days until his classes start. Then Gabe will drive me back to the City just in time to pack more duffels and leave again for one more craptacular semester in Rhode Island, before flying to Spain. Anthony offers them sandwiches, a gesture they appreciate as much as Gideon and I did. I think we all feel mature just because Anthony was thoughtful. Don't ask me why.

I look closely at Gabe's distant eyes through his glasses, my very best friend on this strange planet since the second grade. I haven't seen him in four days, our longest absence since summer began. "How art thou, homie?" I ask.

He looks away blankly. "I need cigarettes," he says in his stale, dry-throat voice.

"I need more aspirin," Gideon says. I nod agreement.

"Yeah, we need drinks, too," Lucas says. "It's hot out. Follow me to the gas station."

"I'm gonna ride with Gabe," Anthony decides, which makes Gideon laugh. "What?" he asks, sensitive and irritated again.

"It's cool, Ant," Gideon says. "We kinda figured you guys would wanna be together."

Gabe and Anthony were roommates at college in Philly this past year, which is the main reason we all started chilling again when the summer arrived. When Gabe isn't with me, he's with Anthony. And when Gabe isn't with Anthony, he's probably lost in a gutter somewhere with his pants around his ankles. Not really. That's just the running joke Anthony and I have about Gabe's vagabond personality. July 4th weekend the two of them went to a party on Long Island and ended up on the beach in Montauk sleeping huddled together behind a huge piece of driftwood. Of course, Gideon and I called them gay; it's required by law to make fun of two dudes crashing together on a beach, even though neither of us care if they actually are gay. Gideon would probably just want to watch, anyway.

In front of Gabe's Mazda, the metallic shell of the SNET payphone reflects the harsh sun. I stare at it hard, lost in my mind for the trillionth time, contemplating the dramas of my family tree. *Should I call my father before we hit the road?* Somebody owes somebody a big apology. I can't tell if I owe Dad an apology, or if he owes me one, or if Grandma owes us both a massively gargantuan *"Oops. Sorry,"* a posthumous care package neither of us will ever receive. I hear Gideon's voice scream "SHOTGUN!" as he races toward the passenger side of the Rover. I forget about the payphone.

Sometimes you feel disappointed when you don't get shotgun and wish it occurred to you to scream it first. Today I'm content to sit in the plush leather rear of the new Rover, watching the back of my friends' heads pushing over the asphalt, their hair whistling, grass-like. The windows are down and the sunroof is open to the cosmos. Lucas gives Gabe vague directions, a flurry of highways Gabe can't possibly remember, promising to stay close on the road. And we're off, the beginning of relentlessness under a noon-blue prism of sky. I even brought four of my Famously Bad Mix Tapes. We're going in style.

THE RANGE ROVER

A ROAD TRIP MUST GIVE YOU A false sense of intimacy, because all of the sudden I feel super excited to see Lucas again, forgetting the fact that I really don't know him much at all. Back in eighth grade, Lucas was just the kid whose Dad owned a big sleepaway camp in New Hampshire. I remember Gabe's mom convincing me to go with him so that Gabe wouldn't feel lonely. I've only seen Lucas once this entire summer on Gideon's balcony. The summer has felt like a lifetime. Ivy League semesters are amazingly short; the summers in between stretch out like accordions. I don't mind. After Sophie dissed me at the start of fall semester, I decided I'd only go to Providence one week out of the year as long as they'd hand me my expensive degree (the one that will make people assume I'm intelligent before I even open my mouth, an asset I am looking forward to exploiting tremendously in real life, whenever it gets here).

Lucas was out in LA, living with his uncle for most of the summer. His girlfriend was out there too, and his life was well set-up in that hazy Southern California style, the style I got a long glimpse of last summer living with Sophie's family. (I developed a cheesy nostalgia for Los Angeles in three weeks of domestic experimentation with Sophie. While Lucas talks about his summer I get lost again in my own sitcom rerun—the tranquil hours in Sophie's little car on the 10 and the 101, my attempts to show Sophie how to meditate on the beach in Malibu, those skinny palm trees balanced impossibly against the sky, the foamy Pacific which is the exact same H20 as the Atlantic but shades itself so differently, the tangly curls of Sophie's hair sweeping against my chin, and Sophie's voice near the end of our time together telling me about a Godard film she wants to watch with me, and me, still hopelessly in love, pretending the film doesn't sound pretentious).

Gideon starts cracking jokes about the enormous potbelly Lucas drank his way into over the past few years out in Wisconsin. "Cocaine is supposed to keep you *skinny*, kid. What happened?"

"Fuck you, bitch," Lucas answers.

On the crackling playback of Side A of my Famously Bad Mixtape #1, Bob is singing about Lily, Rosemary, and the Jack of Hearts, and our voices go silent for a while. The highway churns conveyor-like beneath the tires, screaming down East between the parted trees on the Merritt Parkway, each pair of trees like goal posts, and us continuously scoring.

"Why're you driving behind Gabe?" I ask.

"You think he's nervous about driving?" Lucas answers, laughing a sloppy, uncontained laugh. The thought of Gabe just getting his license now, at 21, is comical to Lucas, and it's also somehow funny to me and Gideon, the two hypocrites who can't get ourselves anywhere alone. "I'm letting him set the pace," Lucas shrugs. I look over his shoulder at the speedometer. We're going a little less than 70mph. "If I was in front, I'd forget about him and go 90 and lose their asses. Look at them in there. Look at Ant with his hand out the window, with that cigarette, all cosmopolitan. What do they even talk about?" Lucas waves at them, then slaps the steering wheel.

"Man," I say. "I don't know how Anthony could stand living with Gabe. I mean I love him, of course, but he gets crazily annoying. I told Gabe a couple of weeks ago on the balcony— you were there, Gideon—that he's the kind of person that only ten people in the world like, and everyone else hates. No middle ground. But those ten people love the shit out of him."

"I knew this kid at my school last year," Gideon says. "He graduated, but we used to call him Moose, for no apparent reason. Let's call Gabe Moose."

"Moose," Lucas repeats, cracking up. Gabe is the exact opposite of Moose-nature: 5'8", pudgy, and cute. There's no bulging athleticism in him; he's ragged and intellectual and a wannabe poet like me. He rocks a five-dollar gray Goodwill blazer that carries the stains of every night since we got home in May. He grew his hair long this year, and grew a mustache and a long goatee that his face wasn't quite ready for. I started calling him Confucius and he eventually got the point, I guess. He cut his hair and shaved a few weeks back, and he looks smooth again, awkwardly handsome in the way he frowns when he disagrees with you, which is always.

I think about the name for a minute. "His Native American name will be Little Moose on a Tirade," I decide. They start cracking up. That kid goes on some tirades. I'll try to explain his mind:

◆

First, Gabe doesn't know how to cross the street. He just hasn't gotten any better at it since we met on the first day of 2nd grade (after he got left back a year, when he stapled his fingers together and cackled at our terrified teacher). Most kids who grow up in the West Village learn how to jaywalk by the time they're about four. You get the timing down, there's a rhythm, and after that city stoplights are only meaningful to cars and tourists. But Gabe made it all the way through an urban childhood without picking up this skill. Even now, when he has the green light, he freezes right in the middle of the Ave like a deer in headlights.

Next month, he's going to Europe for the whole year, where every city has a different system of stoplights, and I truly fear for his life. I'm going to study in Madrid in January and have vowed to visit him regularly in London, committing to a semester with two goals in mind 1) improving my Spanish and 2) keeping Gabe alive. He'll have to survive until I get there.

Most people try to write stream of consciousness as an exercise. Gabe tries to *speak* streamofconsciousness, aka streamofgabe, any time we speak about a cerebral subject, which is often. Exactly six percent of the time he has something amazing to say, and the other 94% I just want to shoot myself. That's a tough stat for a best friend who sleeps on your futon all the time. Sometimes he'll argue with you even when you agree with him, not to play devil's advocate (that'd make way too much sense), but just because he doesn't take the time to breathe and see there's nothing to argue about, which would be a heartbreaking discovery for him. Lack of argument pretty much equals nonexistence to Gabriel Catronas. He was the first person I'd seen in the City when I got back for the summer in May.

Our old high school friend Damien was performing at Nuyoricans Poet's Café, with a featured timeslot and everything. So we rolled with Amelia into Alphabet City. Damien was a year ahead of Gabe, Amelia and I, and he often chilled with us back in the day, mostly during his senior and our junior year, when the Wannabe Poet's Brigade was in its infancy, occasionally sharing stanzas from his notebook and rambling freestyles with Gabe and me. I guess every progressive private school class has a few kids like Damien, popular boys of color who make their white friends feel just a little less white and just a little more down, even if Damien was actually a linguistic nerd, far from invincible and probably only even "cool" by the awkward standards of Quaker school. He probably got jumped more than I did in Junior High.

Damien is currently blowing up into a bonafide poetic success, with his own chapbook (for real) and a fearless stage voice that gives you the instant impression you should've been listening to him since long before whenever you started listening. Amelia says Damien might even be in a PBS documentary about contemporary New York poetry and spoken word.

About thirty kids from our high school showed up for the reading, so it was a bit of a reunion, and we all left feeling electric, like creativity was a genuine possibility in this world, even if it was just vicarious creativity for now. But then Gabe's ADD footsteps took over, and the night got all types of dysfunctional in a hurry. We spent approximately four minutes apiece in about 16 different neighborhoods, until Amelia yelled at Gabe on West Houston Street "Pick a spot and fuckin' stay there, Gabe!" before storming off in the other direction. Gabe and I ended up alone at some jazz club on Hudson Street two blocks from where his parents used to live. It wasn't my style. Gabe thought it was his style when we got there but within 45 minutes he said, "Let's get the fuck outta here."

On the subway he went off on a streamofgabe tirade without any pause or audible punctuation about how he couldn't stand those white musicians usurping a black art form and I weakly tried to spout my own naive idealism instilled in me by years of fancy progressive education intermingled with a growing understanding of dharma about how people are people and identity's one fat construct anyway and also that two white kids don't have much business talking about usurping anything from anyone and he just frowned even though I know he totally agreed with me and then he went off again on another tirade recycled from Spring Break with that *très* annoying frown out of his thin-lipped mouth about race and identity, and I thought he was constructing a poem, some derivative *Song of Himself* in front of me, because he was just chewing through words like Pac-Man chased by ghosts, as if the purpose wasn't to say something but to *have said* something, as if he who has uttered the most words aloud at the time of death gets a big-old trophy, and he went on and on about Manifest Destiny and kept going, going, roaring, coughing that smoker's cough occasionally (which didn't meld well into his free-form monologue) and I stopped trying to interject anything and instead stared up at all the funny ads in the subway, thinking the lack of dialogue might slow him down, like without an equal and opposing force he might chill the fuck out or something, but Gabe wasn't even speaking to me anymore, so I rested my head against a metal pole and watched the dark subway tunnels exploding into the light of each new station as we headed to my mom's Park Slope apartment, where Gabe's favorite futon was waiting for him, knowing there was no off button, no mute, no pause, no fast forward, that sleep was the only thing that could end his tirade.

I guess you have to fish for those polished stones of wisdom from your own murky stream, and that requires endlessly welcoming the muddy waters outward through mouth and pen. To you the entire dull-turquoise rush of your stream makes a kind of cozy sense, but for others it's only about those polished stones, and only if you place them perfectly in the palm of their hands, and even then, only if people aren't too distracted with themselves to notice. And how can I hold Gabe's stream against him when I've got my own?

◆

Our two cars enter a long tunnel. We figure it's probably Gabe's first tunnel with a license, and we feel anticipation. People always get excited about the first time this-or-that happens, all the different micro-losses of virginity that collectively mark some macro rite of passage. None of us have many obvious virginities left at this point, so we celebrate boring little ones. Daylight explodes as we come out the tunnel's other side and Lucas cheers, honks and waves at Gabe, who looks thoroughly confused in the Mazda's rearview. Somewhere outside Hartford, Lucas compliments the songs I put on my Famously Bad Mix

Tape #3, an unblendable blend of Leonard Cohen and Pharcyde, Raekwon and Nina Simone, along with other misfits. Amelia complains that I'm a horrible dj, without any sense of pace or shifts or narrative arc. She got extra mad at me for putting Pharcyde's "Ya Mama," on the mix right after Leonard Cohen's "Lover, Lover, Lover." I tried to tell her music is all about sparking moments, not melodies, and a good moment can exist outside time discontinuously, next to other moments that it has nothing to do with, and that she shouldn't be so linear about a mix tape anyway. She told me I was way too philosophical to ever be a decent dj, and that I should stick to being the CEO of the Wannabe Poets' Brigade.

In Hartford we switch highways and head for Massachusetts.

"We're goin' to camp!" Gideon shouts, stretching his arms up through the sunroof.

"You ever went to sleepaway camp?" Lucas asks him.

"I went one year when I was mad young," Gideon answers.

"Didn't like it?" Lucas asks. Lucas is a huge fan of the entire camp genre, since he practically grew up at his father's.

"It was all right," Gideon shrugs.

"Man," Lucas says, "I don't even see how anyone could not like camp. I mean, I didn't like it either sometimes, but looking back, all you do is *play*. All day you just play. That's all there is to it. Just play. That's all you fuckin gotta *do*." Lucas laughs and slaps Gideon's shoulder in camaraderie. I hear what both of them are saying. I liked camp sometimes, but I always hated people telling me *how* to play. I really didn't even like Camp Winnisquam that much. Don't tell Lucas or Anthony I said that. The summer before I went here, I went to an artsy-fartsy camp in Maine, which was coed and much cooler, not to mention the site of my first kiss. At least there won't be any counselors to tell us what to do now. We are going to camp. And it will be ours.

We stop quickly for fast food, because the little sandwiches that big Anthony made were more symbolic than filling. Anthony takes over driving for Gabe and their car lags behind us now. Our ride enters the space of silence and boredom. I try to meditate, focusing on my breath and the holy-cow smell of expensive leather and the emerald tones behind the windshield. But that only lasts a few minutes before I conclude that it's ridiculously pretentious to meditate in a luxury SUV with two guys watching you in the rearview, wondering what the hell you are doing.

"I know a good car game," I say. Gideon and Lucas perk up.

I admit, I am tremendously proud of this game. Sophie and I came up with it together last summer on the roads of Southern California, but honestly, I did most of the work. When she dissed me back in Providence, I wrote her an angry email claiming all trademarks and copyrights to the car game in our collegiate divorce. I'll describe the game in detail so that you can use it the next time you're on the road with a few people. I don't have a name for it, but if someone asks you can just call it Alex Bardo's Car Game or something, and make royalty checks out to me.

The playing field is anything written external to the environment of your own car. Any text you find on any sign, any other car, on license plates, or anywhere else, as long as it's not in or on your own car, is fair game. You have to go through the alphabet and find a word or some writing that starts with each letter. The first person to make it through the entire alphabet wins. If it doesn't sound exciting, try it. Oh, by the way, there are three passes that each person gets to use, which means that you don't have to find a word that begins with the letter, you just have to find a word that has that letter in it. So, for example, when you get up to X, you don't have to find a sign that says Xylophone or Xavier. You can choose to use a pass and just claim eXit as your X. Also, only one person gets to use each individual text and it goes to whoever calls it out first.

For example, when me and Gideon are both up to Q, he notices AlbuQuerQue written in tiny font on the side of an 18-wheeler we pass and he yells "Albuquerque!" at the top of his lungs before I can see it. The move costs one of his passes (but using a pass on Q makes a lot of sense, if you need some strategy), and he goes on to R. Now he's hooked up, because he's over the hump of Q but I still face that major obstacle, and I slap him on the back of the head in the heat of the moment for calling it out before me. I'm really not a violent person; that's just how intense this game gets. Sophie almost poked my eye out on the Pacific Coast Highway and then almost crashed us through a fence and into the ocean while playing this game, so be careful. The level of competition depends on how generally observant the players are, and we all have perfect vision. The driver is usually at a bit of a disadvantage because he has to focus on the road, but Lucas stays right with me and Gideon. We are finally over our hangovers, enveloped in playtime.

On the Massachusetts turnpike the signs look like Thanksgiving pilgrims, with those 17th-century hats, and I call out from the holograms passing words like Auburn, Best, Craft, Delaware, Exit, Framingham, and Garage. We turn onto another highway for a stretch, moving through Worcester, Lucas yelling Holden and Gideon calling Hudson, Indian, Jersey, and Keane—J and K are surprisingly hard (Gideon is a lucky motherfucker),— and me trying desperately to keep pace, yelling and grabbing a Maine license plate that begins with an H. It goes on in spurts like that, each of us getting on a roll, finding the signs we need. But I stay a little behind them, both neck and neck. There are times when no letters reveal themselves and each of us wants to stop being open to the present, and we start to miss things. Then a sign snaps you back here, right here, frantic to capture its message. We are on edge in the loveliest way. We scavenge on, onto another highway, finding New England calligraphies to claim as ours, playing, playing, playing.

I am the last person to get a Q, and I almost give up the chase, because Gideon and Lucas are almost through the alphabet. It feels hopeless. But then a truck approaching us on the southbound highway says Quality Bedding and I'm back, because then I take Ralph, Stow, Transit, Use, Vehicle, Wilmington, eXit (pass), all within about 30 seconds. We all are at Z in a few moments, which for us is an anxiety-space roughly equal to sudden death O.T. in the semiotic Superbowl. Seriously, I see the sign for the Work Zone Ahead first, I'm sure I do, but the synapses aren't firing for me quickly enough — I can't link the word Zone together with its intrinsic Z-ness — and Lucas claims it for the win.

I feel drained. Once you get into that strenuously focused mind-set, it takes forever to recover. Lucas turns to me, pumping his fist.

"Let the record show," his voice is disgustingly proud, "that my little University of Wisconsin brain just absolutely *schooled* your Ivy League, Wannabe-Poet's ass at your own game, while I was *driving.*" Gideon and I mutter "fuck" under our breaths for the next half hour.

We turn onto our final interstate, onward to New Hampshire. The numbers change but the Red, White, and Blue shield always sketches the route. We play the game again, another close one, which Gideon wins this time. Forty miles past Manchester we switch onto local roads for a half-hour, pinpointing ourselves gradually toward the destination.

The Range Rover handles the shift onto the two-mile dirt road to Camp like it's floating. Lucas gets excited and starts telling Gideon about the specifics of Camp, which is for boys ages 6 to 14. He lists the different names of the various age groups: Beavers, Commandos, Giants...

"I wanna be a Commando!" Gideon shouts. I was only here for one summer, and the bunks for older boys don't have names, so I never got to be a Commando either. It's definitely the best name. Who the fuck wants to be a Beaver?

"Yeah, that's bunks 22-24. I'll tell my dad when we get there," Lucas says.

"I'm gonna be a Commando!" Gideon says, grinning from ear to ear.

ALEX BARDO'S CAR GAME
The Rules

1. Pick Your Ride.

2. Assemble at least 3 people in a car and head out on one of the highways of planet Earth.

3. Resolve to love everyone in the car completely, even if you just met them or haven't seen them in forever.

4. Make sure the driver is someone who can get a bit excited and still keep their eyes on the road. Otherwise DANGER ensues.

5. Any writing external to the car counts, as long as it is on some sign outside of the body of your car.

6. Go through the alphabet finding a word that begins with each letter. Each piece of writing only goes to the person who calls it first.

7. You are allowed 3 passes during the alphabet, which means you can find a sign that has the letter you are up to in it, rather than a word that starts with that letter.

8. First one to find a Z wins, does victory dance, preferably while a Wu Tang Clan anthem blares over the speakers, warped by bass.

9. The winner should then make fun of the losers, especially if the losers have had a more expensive education.

10. Repeat as necessary.

CAMP

THE ARCHED SIGN THAT READS CAMP WINNISQUAM looks ancient but pristine as the Rover glides under it. Lucas pushes the bangs out of his eyes and starts belting out the camp song. I don't think I've ever heard him sing before, and his voice—which still sounds sloppy and pubescent whenever he speaks—suddenly seems clear as a bell, choral quality. I don't know the song; I wasn't here long enough to learn or care. I'm sure Anthony, who went here almost as many years as Lucas, is singing behind us in Gabe's Mazda. We get out of the car and stretch our legs. A small fold of Lake Winnipesaukee's enormity shines in front of us. Lucas' dad, Carl, rides up on one of the camp's golf carts. Carl never walks anywhere at Camp; even if he's going from one side of a basketball court to the other, he drives his golf cart around the court. He pulls it off like it's his chariot, without seeming lazy at all.

"Hey guys!" He stops the motor. Lucas goes up and gives him a hug and kiss. The four of us walk up together behind Lucas. Mr. Putterman spots Anthony first—he went to camp for the maximum nine years, along with his older brother.

"Anthony," Mr. Putterman says, embracing him like a second son. Carl looks at Gideon with a slight frown and Gideon introduces himself, suddenly putting on a mature and charming manner. Carl takes Gabe's hand but doesn't recognize him. Gabe says: "Gabriel Catronas." Carl smiles softly and says, "Of course, Gabriel, of course," as if he will never forget this name again.

I shove my hand forward, assuming he won't recognize me, and say "Alex Bardo."

Mr. Putterman gives me a sudden look of care and concern, just like my therapist did a few weeks ago as she suggested that I confront my Dad. "How are you, Alex?" Carl asks, taking my hand.

Nobody else had to answer a question, and it catches me by surprise. My brain freezes.

"Um…I don't really know," I say without thinking. After a moment I realize this is the most honest and least acceptable answer to a small talk question. Awkwardness ensues.

Mr. Putterman ignores it and turns back toward the golf cart. He starts telling us about our options for playtime, ticking each choice off on his fingers: There are the basketball courts, the tennis courts, the soccer fields, tether ball *(you might be too old for tether ball,* he says), the rec center *(though who wants to stay inside on such a super-gorgeous day like we're having?* he asks), the waterfront, the ski boat, the sail boats, the obstacle course, and on and on and on. In the middle of his speech, I realize that this is what Carl does; he's a traveling salesman of playtime, with a briefcase full of kayaks. When he isn't at Camp, he's on the road, in New York, Connecticut, Boston, the Philadelphia suburbs, Florida, and even out West in LA and the Bay Area, convincing upper-middle class and wealthy parents to surrender their boys to him for the summer, just to play. He probably doesn't even know how *not* to act like a salesman, and his voice sounds like we're shopping in aisle five of Toys R' Us. That's just his way, even though we're getting everything for free anyway. Gideon thanks him profusely, turning up the charm. Carl sets us up with made beds and towels in bunk 27. That makes us Giants, as indicated by the hand-painted plaque above the doorway. "Yo," Gideon says, disappointed, after Carl drives away on his cart. "I wanted to be a Commando."

Although Camp officially ended two days ago, they're in the middle of a father-son weekend. In this strange ritual, fathers drive up and spend one last weekend living in the bunks with their sons, experiencing firsthand just how expensive it is to send your spoiled boy into third-world living conditions for the summer. When I was 14, Dad came up for the weekend after playing a music gig at a festival in Massachusetts. I felt proud, because a few of the other dads were fans of his music, and a bunch of them played a folk jam session together around a campfire. Dad and I didn't fight at all that weekend, at least not until we stopped for seafood in Connecticut on the long drive home.

We head over to the barbeque on the island camp, where the older boys have their bunks. I follow Anthony and Lucas into one of the small docked motorboats, wondering if it can hold all five of us as it rocks and sags. Lucas eventually gets the motor going and we're off. When we reach the island, he thuds and scrapes the boat into the dock. Gabe loses his balance and almost falls in the water, but Anthony grabs him by the lapel of his Goodwill blazer with a powerful arm, hauling him back in.

We disembark. *Disembark* sounds like a sea captain's term. We *disembark* to the port side. That sounds good to me. Across the field I see the bunk Gabe and I stayed in our summer here. It feels familiar, but not familiar enough for me to get all nostalgic. Only Sophie and Grandma have the power of nostalgia over me, and those are both nostalgias of the papercut-beneath-ribcage variety. Anthony, on the other hand, is standing on the dock, inhaling the entire lake with each breath into his broad chest. This is where his childhood lives, and you can tell it was a mostly good one by just looking at him now. He lingers on the dock as we start to walk across the field, looking back at the huge lake glistening, calmly answering the sun's descent.

"Isn't this gorgeous?" he says as I pass him.

"Yeah man, it's nice," I say, and walk away. I'm not in the mood for more memories. I just wanna play.

We go and play a little ball at the basketball courts and then head for the mess hall, outside of which a bunch of long tables hold all kinds of food. There are steaks, burgers, chicken breasts, salmon fillets, three different pasta salads, beet salad, deviled eggs, and even caviar. Absent are the bug juice and suspect mystery coldcuts, anything I associate with Camp food. I guess Carl needs to put on a show to keep that inflow of playtime-capital coming next summer.

In the center of it all is Graham, the aging Southern man from 'Bama who still runs the older boys' camp. Anthony goes up to him. I follow with Gabe.

"Graham," Anthony calls with confidence. "Anthony Kerrigan. Remember us?" He extends his right hand, which Graham takes as a matter of course, never altering his bulldog expression. All he can say to his former campers is:

"Alright guys. C'mon, let's belly up now." That's how I remember him anyway, that dixie-compassionate-militarism invading the depth of upper New England yankeedom. Gabe and I don't even bother to try to say hello to him after that. We just belly up, like he told us.

The food is good. I put my paper plate down and wrap my arm around Gabe's shoulder on the steps of our old bunk. Gabe doesn't complain about my arm and he doesn't smile, either. Anthony and Lucas wander around and talk to some of the older staff and people who knew them, like Stan Cobb, who comes up every summer from North Carolina to live in the back cottage and run the sailing program. His son is the same age as us. His name was Quent, I think, and he was a great athlete. Quent was 6'3" when we were 14, and I swear I never saw that kid miss a free throw. Automatic, cash, butter, water, skillz, splash in the ocean, whatever you want to call it. Quent's free throws are the only thing I remember about him, and it's heartbreakingly unfair to remember someone just for free throws.

The fathers and sons socialize in parallel universes. I hear one of the fathers say "Clinton," and I assume cynically that he's talking about the President's scandal in relation to his stock portfolio. I look down at the dad's Reeboks, so gleaming and white it might be the first time they've ever been out of the box in his closet. The boys are boys, their baggy summer gear, Gary Payton jerseys, Nike apparel, the usual sweatshop status symbols. Right in front of us, three boys are beating the hell out of a fourth, three feet from an oblivious circle of Dads. They look about twelve. They aren't hurting him badly, but he's trying to fend them off with his lacrosse stick, and they keep coming after him and jumping him. They steal his stick and wrestle him to the ground again and again, mashing his face in the dirt, but he's loving it. He keeps coming back for more, as if his adrenaline is primed by humiliation. I think back on when I was his age, and whether I was the defiant one on the bottom or a part of the wolfpack on top. Honestly, I was probably the witty coward on the sidelines, cracking jokes and yelling "Awwww, shit!", hoping not to be next on the beatdown queue.

[NOTE TO SELF: *You might always be that witty coward. You may have to just accept your karma on that one. Now that you're 21, a real man or some bullshit — writing this down seven months after the fact in a Barcelona hostel — it might be time to assess whether or not you've always been a coward and always will be a coward. It's really possible there's only been one single courageous act in these 21 years, a moment from the first week of Freshman year at college. In this frozen moment, this soundtrack moment, this trophy moment, you go alone to a Rhode Island School of Design party full of Sophomores and Juniors where you only know one person, and it's not Sophie. You walk right up to her next to the stereo, doubtlessly, like your name is Baron von Manhattan. You're really not sure if this even counts as a moment of courage, because courage seems more like a positive presence, and this is more like a mere absence, the absence of the high-school thought that you are not the type of kid who goes up to pretty, thoughtful-looking girls and asks them what they're all about. But the dark eyes of the artist soon-to-be-known as Sophie alight like slow-burning charcoal. She tells you about LA and film and asks what it's like to have a kinda sorta famous folk musician for a father and to have gone to a Quaker school in NYC. Within three days, you two are holding hands all over College Hill. The first time you go down on her you totally forget about the need to make new friends at school. Within two weeks she is planning to come home with you for Thanksgiving, to come uptown with you and Gabe and Amelia and watch them blow up parade balloons by the Museum of Natural History.*]

After the barbeque, we pile onto the large party barge with a bunch of dads and sons and head back to the mainland, not sure what to do with ourselves, surrounded on all sides by 10-year-old boys and middle-aged dudes. One of the last few counselors, one of the stragglers left behind to close up the camp, tells us about a party at this club called Thunder Alley in the next town over.

"Sounds like a gathering of Who's Who in Genetic Birth Defects," Gabe says in his stale voice.

"Let's Go!" Gideon shouts, slapping Anthony and me on the shoulders.

THUNDER ALLEY

WE'RE FROLICKING NAKED IN SHOWER HOUSE B, getting ready for the evening. There's been a lot of naked frolicking with these kids this summer, so it's nothing new, except for the group shower part, the unquestioned homoerotic part of Camp life, the part that traumatizes a late-blooming 14-year-old like I was. Gideon walks around his apartment naked most of the time if his parents are away. Even when he has guests — *especially* when he has guests — he prances with little Giddy just dangling. He doesn't have a special philosophy about nudity or self-expression or anything, he just doesn't seem to have much use for clothing. I saw Anthony and Gabe naked one night in July, which might be the first time I ever saw Gabe naked in 13 years of sleepovers and crashing, if you can believe that.

That was a strange night. I started a conversation with a girl at a party uptown about Curtis Mayfield and Nico and how the '70s were — objectively speaking — better than the '90s, and how everyone is always born exactly 20 years too late. I'm pretty sure, but not certain, that, one subway ride and one long walk later, I started sucking face with this girl downstairs, right in front of Gideon's doorman. But by the time we got up to Gideon's apartment something strange had happened, and I was no longer in the picture. Gideon and Anthony were both naked on Gideon's parents' bed, the girl topless. Now I found myself sitting cross-legged on the floor in the bedroom corner, preferring some meditative voyeurism to participation. Gabe was sitting on the rug across from me, wearing not a thing but his Goodwill blazer.

I'm pretty sure he was masturbating apathetically. I'm also pretty sure I saw Gideon spanking and kissing Anthony, but it was probably just the play of shadows from the street lamps out the window in Washington Square.

"You got a really *nice* ass," Lucas tells Gabe as he wipes soap from his shoulders, laughing. "The symmetry of those buttocks is just *sublime.*"

"You got a really nice *belly.*" Gabe responds. Lucas stops laughing, and turns his attention to Gideon, to try to get the focus off of his weight gain. "Still hasn't grown back yet, huh?" Lucas motions at Gideon's stubbly pubis. Gideon shaved his pubes a few weeks ago in a 4:00am frenzy. He read, probably from a porn magazine, that it adds the illusion of length. Instead, it made him look like a six-year-old.

I put on my minimalist summer uniform, black jeans and a white tee shirt. My sneakers are way past their prime, but they're all I brought with me. Now we're rolling, crowding into the dusty black Mazda, five city boys heading for Thunder Alley. Gabe offers not to drink so he can drive, and I shoot him a look that says, "Who are you and what have you done with my Little Moose?" We grab two 18 packs of beer on the road, and I pop in Alex Bardo's Famously Bad Mix Tape #3. The blend is bad but the beats are good. Lucas cracks a beer in the car and Gideon and I follow his lead, which probably isn't too bright, but we ain't too bright either—we just go to really good schools. Gabe gets us deeply and utterly lost on some back road, start-of-a-horror-movie lost. I'm not even sure if we're still in the United States, but I don't see any Mounties anywhere. Eventually we right our course and find our way to Thunder Alley around 11:00pm.

We stand around Gabe's Mazda in the parking lot and drink beer with the doors open, listening again and again to Nice 'n Smooth's "Sometimes I rhyme slow, Sometimes I rhyme quick", which shamelessly samples the guitar riff from Tracy Chapman's "Fast Car", but they still turned it into a good song, which accounts for the fact that it's the seventh time tonight we've listened to it. (Amelia hates when I play the same song over and over again like this; she claims a good song loses its grace if you play it too much too soon, but I insist that repetition just amplifies the moment's perfection.) We piss in the bushes about four times each and drink about six beers apiece before entering Thunder Alley. I flash my fake Kansas ID and have a moment of future-nostalgia, sad that I'll only need the card for a few more months.

Thunder Alley is classier than I expected. There are three different rooms, one of which seems more like a honky-tonk than the others. I sit down with Gabe and Lucas at the side of the bar in the room that seems the most normal. Lucas, my playtime patron, starts buying me beers, and I start drinking them. Bottles are $1.75, which seems like a ridiculous price. Gideon and Anthony head toward the dance floor in the honky-tonk room, prowling for women.

"There actually are some *cuties* here," Lucas says enthusiastically.

"Yeah, there are also some star-crossed chromosomes," Gabe shrugs, and walks off into a crowd.

I survey the scene to see if there are any girls that have that unnameable look behind their eyes, the one I've only found when I wasn't thinking about it, but I can't see anyone's eyes well, and I'm okay just watching the dark vibrations of bodies.

An MC Hammer song comes on. I cringe, but Lucas just laughs and gets up. Within 90 seconds he starts dancing with what appears to be a beautiful lady. Later it turns out she's from Scotland and works as a laundress at Camp. He comes back a half hour later and says he kissed her on the dance floor. I look over and see her outline across the room: she seems elegant, older and gorgeous, and is now standing with a couple of other dudes. Lucas' claim seems pretty suspect, but I'm not about to call my playtime patron a liar to his face. Gideon and Anthony have no luck, rare for both of them this summer. Gabe gets deep into a conversation with a chubby 30-something blond with a sleeve of tattoos that also coats half her neck, but the chit-chat ends abruptly when she mentions, and I quote: "My man just got out of jail. He was supposed to meet me here an hour ago." Gabe comes over to the bar and laughs it off. Gabe's laughter is a rare gift. I tell him he has to write that one down. He tells me to write it down. I just did.

The lights come on strongly at 1:30am, giving everyone a harsh visual shot of sobriety. We flood out into the parking lot and crowd back into Gabe's car. Lucas looks around nervously. He found out that the Scottish beauty into whose throat he shoved his tongue has a boyfriend at the bar, and moreover, that boyfriend is a counselor at Camp. When our car reaches the dirt road, we see headlights behind us in the deep night. It must be the queen of Scots and her boyfriend returning.

Gideon declares two missions upon our arrival at Camp. First, we have to get Gabe liquored up. He handled responsibility like a trooper and now it's time to reward him with beer, like the veritable wannabe poet he is. Second, Gideon decides we all need some food. The only obstacle is the new overnight security guard Carl hired. We head for the kitchen, Lucas in the lead. The security guard, ironically nicknamed Santa Claus due to a striking resemblance, comes up from the shadows.

Lucas chuckles arrogantly at his presence, and approaches. "Hey, how you doing? I'm Carl Putterman's son An-"

"Back up," Santa says, angrily.

"Excuse me?" Lucas asks.

"Back up," St. Nick repeats. Lucas backs off a couple of feet and repeats:

"I'm Carl Putterman's son. We just wanted to get some food."

"Well, I don't know who you are, but I can't approve something like that. Kitchen's closed. Camp's closed."

The car behind us has arrived and one of the girls—a shorter, thicker friend of the Scottish girl—comes up to us and Santa.

"I know these lads," she says in a thick British accent. Santa Claus lightens up and lets Lucas explain. Lucas drafts a scratch letter assuming full responsibility for opening the kitchen and for any ensuing plagues or tsunamis, and Santa finally opens the padlock for us.

"Why did your Dad hire a security guard?" Anthony asks.

"Counselors kept coming back from nights off drunk, stealing food, and taking canoes out into the middle of the lake and losing them out there. Canoes ain't cheap," Lucas slaps Anthony on the back. "Let's go steal some food."

London Denise follows us inside. I can't decide if she wants to chill with us or if she's just making sure we don't piss in the lemonade dispenser. Gideon starts flirting with her, half seriously, half for his own amusement. Lucas keeps asking how Gail, the Scottish beauty, feels about him. "Did she say anything to you about me?" Apparently, while grinding on the dance floor to "2 Legit 2 Quit", Lucas fell deeply in love. That's how it goes sometimes. Denise avoids his questions.

Meanwhile, me and Gabe reheat masses of camp pizza in one of the microwaves while Anthony and Gideon hurl scoops of strawberry ice cream at each other in the walk-in freezer. Anthony wields the metal scoop like a mini lacrosse stick, pelting Gideon's face with merciless and uncanny accuracy. Gideon tries to convince Denise to go into the freezer with him, practically the only setting Gideon hasn't messed around with a girl in this summer. There have been girls in his parents' vacant bed, girls on breezy balconies, girls on grimy park benches, girls on highrise roofs, girls in Amtrak bathrooms, girls pressed against the sandwich counter of Happy's Village Deli, Canadian girls, girls on muddy beaches, girls in mildewed basements, but no girls in walk-in freezers, yet.

"I'm druuuuunnnkkk," Gideon drawls, pushing forward the bangs of his Caesar haircut. He accidentally spits in the vat of strawberry ice cream, while dabs of the ice cream that Anthony hurled at him dry into sticky goo on his cheeks.

Lucas keeps trying to pump information out of London Denise about her friend Gail, who Denise claims is her very best mate (apparently intimacy comes easily after months of cleaning the nervous stains out of little boys' underwear together). All Denise has to say is that Gail's boyfriend doesn't like Lucas, because in Denise's words "He saw you try to kiss her," to which Lucas responds that he didn't *try* anything, that he had fully *succeeded*, that faces had been properly and thoroughly sucked over in Thunder Alley.

"He thinks you're just a spoiled rich brat," she says, avoiding eye contact.

We instantly jump to Lucas' defense with shouts of "Whoa, Whoa, Whoa!" He can't help the fact that his mother remarried a real estate developer and moved him out of the City into the richest town in America for high school, or that he has a whole guest house to himself or drives a new Range Rover, the latest emotional peace treaty with his mother (according to Anthony's version of the story). I decide on the spot that 1) Lucas is the patron of playtime, 2) if playtime doesn't have patrons then this strange planet will become an even darker place, 3) Lucas is now my *boy,* and that most importantly 4) I will defend my boys against all criticisms, especially true criticism.

It doesn't matter, because Denise says the Scot's boyfriend is headed back to wherever in the Midwest it is that he's from tomorrow to finish Grad school. We make tentative plans to meet up with the laundresses tomorrow night. We take the rest of the beer back to our bunk, Lucas reminding us to be quiet because of the fathers and sons still in bunks on either side of us. We get into bed and whisper loudly about the summer, and the gorgeous Scottish and not-so-gorgeous British laundresses, and whatever else fills the dark void in front of us. For about a half-hour we have a heated discussion about varying perspectives on U.S. motivations in the bombings of Hiroshima and Nagasaki — don't ask how we get on that topic after 10 beers and a few shots apiece, but suffice it to say that in the true style of our vagabond intellectualism we profess both the classical and revisionist interpretations of history with insightful clarity—Gideon takes a pro-U.S. stance because that's what he's been taught, I take the radical stance about imperialism and multinational this-and-that because that's where my head is at, and Gabe screams incoherent ramblings at the bunk beds, streamofgabe-ing about love and truth and suffering because he's our Little Moose on a Tirade. I look up at the obscure wooden plank of the top bunk. Our voices fade one by one, coming back to make a quiet funny comment, and then silence again. I pass out, cozy among comrades, falling way down under layers of dreams I won't remember.

THE DAYTIME LAKE

MY WATCH SAYS 11:04AM WHEN MY EYES open. I check my internal hangover meter. I feel medium-well done.

I look over and Gabe is huddled in his bunk, scribbling in his notepad, writing furiously, frowning upward at the page.

"Wannabe Poets Brigade," I say, yawning. That's the name of our old writerly clique, by the way, a name our favorite English teacher gave us in high school. He was trying to cut us down to size, but I loved it and would leave haikus on the blackboard for him every morning, signed "- WPB." I always took the name as a compliment, thinking that "wannabe" is about as close to perfection as you can get anyway, but Gabe was a purist, and at first took it as an insult to his craft. After high school, when the nostalgia overtook his pride, he embraced the moniker.

Gabe ignores me and keeps writing. I fish through my duffel and grab an aspirin, dry swallowing it.

"Come on, man," Anthony whips Gabe with a sweaty beach towel, way more alive than we are. "It's Playtime."

The morning is all about basketball. The air is hot and dry again, and we all go skins, flexing our muscles at the four rows of empty metallic seats courtside. Right after lunch I cannonball into the lake off of the docks, forgetting about the rule that you have to wait a half hour after eating or you might get a cramp and spontaneously combust in the water. The vast lake feels like it's a living being, healing and refreshing after the claustrophobic heat of ball. I let it hold me for a while, groundless, just slightly beyond time's reach. In the afternoon we play more basketball.

Lucas and Anthony start trash talking, and the game quickly gets macho and edgy. I go up for a rebound and come down on Lucas' foot and turn my ankle over. It hurts like crazy and for a moment I think they may have to amputate. It's the second time this summer I've twisted that ankle. My sneakers are old and worn out, offering no ankle support. The only other pair of shoes I own, left in NYC, are also way past their prime. I guess I believe that if my shoes are worn-in, I will look either like I have been, am, or am going somewhere. I could easily ask my dad for a new pair, but I refuse. My magazine internship this summer was unpaid except for a meal stipend, and Grandma's inheritance only covers school expenses for now, so I am a broke-ass poet of the wannabe variety, and that's my preference anyway.

Anthony gets me some ice. Within five minutes, my ankle looks like there's a tennis ball lodged under the skin. The color is uneven, ranging from purplish blue to midnight tones. He helps me limp back to our bunk. I sit down at the one desk in the corner and tell him I'll be fine. I try to meditate, but my mind is chock full of ache and distraction. I read for a while. I have two books with me: one on poststructuralism, and a book my father gave me by his Buddhist teacher called *Crazy Wisdom*. I read that one, figuring I could use a lot more of both those things.

I hear the guys' voices coming back to the bunk around 5:00pm and hobble outside to greet them. I realize that the bunks around us have gone silent, that all the fathers and sons departed Camp while I was absorbed in reading. A memory hits me, one which was never very memorable until now:

I am 14, at the end of this very weekend, and Dad is loading my two duffels, tennis racket, deflated basketball and his three guitars and banjo into the back of his yellow tank-like Volvo. I climb in shotgun and insist we listen to hip hop at least for the first hour, my old cracked 3rd Bass cassette to be precise. Dad scowls at this suggestion, without saying no to my demand.

He turns the ignition, breathes, and unleashes an almost violent sigh, sighing like life is a burden he can't possibly verbalize to a teenager. This makes me roll my eyes at him dramatically, rolling my eyes like life is a game I can't possibly teach to a 45-year-old.

The dirt road crackles and spits pebbles under our tires. Camp drops away behind me, home for the past two months. I am going to start high school in a few weeks. At least Gabe will be coming with me, all the way across the East River to Brooklyn Heights! I'm sure high school will be better than what came before, better than 8th grade, and better than this Camp. Dad and I will not argue until we stop for seafood in Connecticut. I can't remember what starts the fight, but by the time we hit the FDR drive I am insisting on sleeping at Grandma's apartment.

◆

Anthony taps me gently on the shoulder, mercifully pulling me out of my thoughts. "You want to get some food?" I hobble after him.

We go to the country store down the road to get sandwiches on the camp's credit line, and lots of beer for later. I split a turkey hero with Anthony and we buy another 30-pack for the night. The girl behind the counter looks about 16 and is extremely cute with her simple jeans and light tee, long brown hair and hazel eyes. Lucas takes the fact that she doesn't card him for the beer as a sign that she's into him.

"Fuck," he says back in the Rover. "We should've asked her what she was doing later. She could've come to Camp with us."

"She was like 12, you pedophile-in-training," Gabe says.

"Fuck you, Little Moose. What're you, nuts? She was at least 18."

"Is this why you're still dating a high school girl, because you just can't tell how old they are?"

Lucas punches Gabe in the shoulder as hard as he can. Gabe crumples for a moment, but doesn't punch back. He rises up, laughing a rare laugh full of sarcasm and victory, the harshest form of retaliation. "Well, even if she was a little young, it's the best thing around here," Lucas chuckles.

"I got my woman for this trip, and she ain't twelve," Anthony says with quiet pride, raising his arm over his head and stretching it over Gabe's deadened shoulder. Anthony has a lady from Hong Kong waiting for him in Ithaca. I should speak of Anthony's travels, if for no other reason than that I admire him for not pretending it's even an option to stay still:

Anthony is indeed the Traveling Man; his mind is perfectly suited to motion. I've been fascinated by him all summer and wonder why we weren't closer in 8th grade. I've never seen anyone absorb the medium of his experience as much as Anthony does. (Yes, I stole that line from Burroughs. Won't be the last line stolen today, either.) He'll see a painting and want to paint, and not just paint, but learn to paint in the exact style of that painter. He'll see an indie movie and want to follow in the footsteps of the protagonist. He'll see a pride of lions on a nature show on PBS and one of two phenomenal responses will come from his lips: he'll either want to become one of the people who studies lions, or he'll want to be one of the lions themselves. I actually heard him say on Gideon's balcony, completely honestly, "I wish I was a mother lion." He'll learn about a global injustice and focus on researching it for a whole day, then forget about it completely. This instantaneously obsessive personality could be taken as erratic and naive, but Anthony gives it such hopefulness that it's at least a little heroic. Something new will always come up for him, so each interest rises, gets registered, and then placed back down on the path.

His mom works for an airline, which means he gets plane tickets for next to nothing, so travel is a given. His older brother once flew from JFK to London just for a day, just to buy a specific type of leather jacket.

In July, Anthony traced the entire circumference of the globe. At the time of his trip, Anthony was trying to get over the loss of his perfect lady a few months before, this girl from Dubai who went to school with him in Philly and was tied into some serious heiress-type wealth. Of course, her Muslim parents wouldn't want her sleeping with anyone, and much less an anyone who was half Irish and half Russian Jew. So they met up three times over the Spring in her family's elaborate London flat. The second time, Anthony surprised her when he knew she'd be there, calling her from the pay phone on the street corner and telling her to look out the window. It was exactly like any cheesy movie, only when you actually pull off the cheesy movie, it's no longer cheesy. We all thought it was pretty smooth, and judging by Anthony's description of the sex, she thought it was pretty smooth too.

The next time he visited the Dubai girl her energy had shifted — one of those shifts that make you think reality is just a trap door leading to outer space — just like Sophie when we got back to Providence after our time together in LA. In May, the Dubai girl left Anthony standing near Picadilly Circus, broken-souled. She couldn't escape the obstacle of her family, so in place of a burdensome union, she just left him standing on the street in somebody else's city. It's bad enough to be left standing on the street in a city you know well.

When he told me about her, I was sitting on the balcony at Gideon's place, lounging in the hammock that I slept in whenever I didn't feel like going home, watching evening crowds move under the Washington Square Arch across the street. It was a Friday night in June, the moment in the City's weekly narrative when everyone forgets their disappointments and convinces his- or herself that something transcendent or at least shiny might, finally, happen *tonight*. I took a long gulp of the forty from Happy's Village Deli a few blocks away. I felt full of a carbonated sadness that was part Anthony's, and part mine.

I could see Anthony in London, broad, handsome and defeated on what I wrongly pictured as a cobblestone street, watching his lady drift back into the labyrinth, then not watching her because he didn't want her to turn and see him watching her.

What he needed to cure his broken heart was more travel. On his trip around the world in July, he ended up going to Hong Kong for a week and meeting another extremely rich girl (her father owned some four-star hotel there), who happened to be headed into her Senior year at Gideon's school in Ithaca. He spent four fervent days with her, and promised to see her if he ever visited Gideon. Hong Kong and Ithaca are strange places for romance, but Anthony is a Traveling Man and heiress-magnet, and that means that you find your love in random spots.

◆

We frolic in Shower House B again, erupting into spontaneous haiku and jokes about laundresses. Lucas has already made plans to chill with London Denise, the larger laundress, tonight, hoping she'll bring along the other one, his new Scottish love. We find a sheltered gazebo on the lakefront, a ways down from the last of the younger boys' bunks. I don't remember this gazebo from my season at Camp, and I quickly decide that it's one of my favorite locations on this strange planet. The vast lake hums right in front of us, unfolding beyond the inlet. After two days I am near convinced that the lake is a type of sentient being, way more sentient than either the Atlantic or Pacific. Whatever is the opposite of claustrophobia, that's what I feel by its side. We have our 30-packs in the kitchen fridge (Santa Claus doesn't give us any trouble) and we bring beers waterside in handfuls and pocketfuls. The two laundresses come and sit with us in the gazebo, soberly awkward and nervous. They sip cheap, boxed wine out of Dixie cups. For a moment I wonder what brought them here, across the pond to rural New Hampshire to wash boys' underwear. Is this place a resume builder for them? A great adventure? The only job they could find?

The Scottish beauty gives me a sip of her wine. Hints of antifreeze, vinegar, and grape juice swish around in my mouth. It reminds me of the Chinese restaurant uptown near Grandma's old apartment that serves free wine with meals, the one that has been getting Gabe and I socially lubricated since we were 15. The only time Gabe and I went there this summer, the night ended 80 blocks downtown at 3:00am in a pizza parlor on St. Marks Place, with Gabe climbing up on the counter and demanding free pizza. He figured the place was about to close and they would just throw out the leftovers, that there was enough food in the city to feed everybody for free, and that he was a wannabe poet, which was enough vocation to earn a free slice. When they wouldn't give him the one that looked a little past its prime, he started protesting, turning into the Cesar Chavez of Sicilian slices. He dropped his Salvation Armani pants down to his ankles and shouted "You fascist!" (he drops his pants a lot these days. I think it's representational). The owner picked up the phone and started to call the police and I got Gabe out of there.

In the gazebo, the conversation darts back and forth between us like one of those tiny, spot-colored, rubber balls that rattles and zips off of every surface and only stops when it wants to. The laundresses seem to think our particular brand of low-brow-high-brow humor is endearing, even though we keep making references they can't understand—references to the summer, to NYC culture, to 8th grade romance. Gabe tells the British one, Denise, that he's going to London for the year, trying to strike up a conversation with her about the UK, but it doesn't really work. Anthony finds out that Gail, the Scottish one (she is 25, beautiful, intelligent, and waayyyy the hell out of our leagues), studied several years ago in Dublin, which is where he is headed for his study abroad. Anthony tries to strike up a conversation about Ireland, mentions that he's half Irish, but that doesn't work either. The only people we can really talk to are the various counselors, soon to be leaving camp, wandering down from the darkness toward the lake. A few of them are younger than us, which makes me feel eerily old at 20.5. We offer them beer and seats. Some accept and stay for a little while, mixing voices with half-smoked cigarettes. Some decline and pass on.

Gail disappears suddenly to bed, with just a whisper of goodnight. If Lucas really kissed her last night, it's pretty clear there won't be a repeat performance. Eventually, Anthony and Gideon get bored, but not before they find out from Denise where Gail sleeps, and also that the laundry girls live in the same cabin as the garbage girls. Anthony and Gideon go off on the prowl again, in search of a garbage-laundry girl orgy, or else just someone new to talk to now, or someone new to talk *about* later. Lucas, Gabe, and London Denise all go up to the camp kitchen. I am left alone in the gazebo, breathing with the darkness. I sip my fifth beer, listening to, more than looking at, the abysmal rustling of the lake.

◆

I start thinking about this story I read earlier in the summer, *The Aleph* by Jorge Luis Borges. If you haven't read it, I highly recommend it. I've read it about a dozen times now. Gabe says Jorge is played out already, a postcolonial sellout, and the one Comp Lit professor I actually like said that Jorge is widely considered a European apologist, but I hope I'm past the age where it's not cool to like things just because alternative-minded people critique them. Rebelling against whatever's mainstream, trying to perfectly *niche* yourself all the time, just seems like a recipe for loneliness. Besides, worrying about postcolonial apologies at an Ivy League institution seems a bit, um, ironic. When I read *The*

Aleph for the first time, it was as if my man Jorge hit me with some megaton warhead of insight. It left me reeling, because it was all about Sophie, except in the story, Sophie's name is Beatriz. My man Jorge gets real deep into the illusory nature of reality and the inconceivability of the universe, and finally in the story he receives the entire universe as a pocket-sized gift, but that's just a little side plot. Really, the whole thing is a love story, an after-the-fact love story.

Beatriz, who Jorge obviously loved dearly, has died before her time (a meaningless statement, but you get the point). Each year on her birthday, Jorge goes to her house to pay his respects to her father and her cousin. On one visit, 11 years after she's died, Jorge sees a huge portrait of her on the wall, and he goes up to it and says (and I even *heard* his voice as I read the story the first time, slow and fatherly, which never happens to me when I read): "Beatriz, Beatriz Elena, Beatriz Elena Viterbo, beloved Beatriz, Beatriz lost forever, it's me, Borges."

The fact that Jorge used his real name in the story makes me love him that much more. I would never do that. I can picture the gravity on his face and the saturation in his chest, that un-clingy desperation, not wanting anything except to know that a fucking painting remembers him. (I finally figured out why people stare at pictures. These past few years, I've become an expert picture-starer. It's not because you miss the person. It's because you miss the memory. You stare at a picture because you want to make sure that your own damn memory remembers you back, to make sure your projections reciprocate all the effort you put into projecting them. How messed up is that?)

The other part of *The Aleph* worth mentioning is that during a visit, Beatriz' cousin shows Jorge the Aleph itself, a small portal in his basement that allows the viewer to witness every event in the universe from every possible perspective, simultaneously. The story is magical realism, which obviously allows a writer to do way more than a writer should be allowed to do (which is why magical realism was invented). But for about two pages, Jorge attains literary enlightenment, as he describes what he sees when he peers into the Aleph, which is everything, everywhere, everyone, everyway. By the end of the story, Jorge knows the whole damn universe, including his reader—which is you, which is me—but even after all that amazement, he's still just thinking about Beatriz in the end.

It must be the lake—its darkness, its depth, its intimate hugeness—that makes me think of the Aleph now. Now I'm struck hard, recalling twin memories with Sophie again. The memories hit my throat and chest with a force I haven't felt since the winter, when I was home for the holidays and my therapist said I was grieving. Her mouthing the word *grieving* put me in a crazily defensive mood, and I told her that you can only grieve for dead people, and I wasn't even grieving for Grandma anymore, that I was over it by then. She said, "A) That's bullshit, and you know it Alex, and B) We don't just grieve the dead. We grieve anytime a relationship shifts, anytime any of our attachments aren't what they once were. Grief is much bigger than you think. Walk down the street when you leave my office, and you'll immediately see that every single person is grieving." I said, "Whatever."

The first memory that hits is of Sophie when our relationship is at its prime. It's early 1997, and we are hibernating together every February day and night, annoying everyone who knows us or passes us on the Providence street. In this memory, we're curled up on the tiled floor of the handicapped bathroom in my claustrophobically fluorescent dorm at school. An hour ago we ate magic mushrooms—they're just kicking in beyond the initial stomach ache—and we're examining the individual squares of tile below with peaceful awe. After a while I get bored of the floor and start watching Sophie watch the floor, sketching her hands across it. I love watching people watch things. If I go to a movie with someone, I spend half the time watching the person watch the movie. Watching things directly gets boring quickly.

Watching people watch things never gets old. I begin to run my long fingers over Sophie's hands and up her arms. Suddenly she turns and looks right at me, eyes fierce. This memory becomes rosier as time goes by, so nauseatingly first-love it'd make you sick if I could draw it for you. Sophie's pupils are enormous and black from the hallucinogens. There is so much clarity about who she wants to be, and so much confusion about who she actually is. And that shit has got me hooked.

That memory, that handicapped-bathroom-floor-stare, always makes me smile doofily.

The second memory is the harsh aftertaste of the first. Now it's August 23, 1997, 6:20am Pacific time, one year to the day before this lakeside gazebo, at my gate at LAX. I've been staying with Sophie and her family in Benedict Canyon for three whole weeks at the end of summer, a bold adult move for both of us. Since I was a little kid, I've never even spent three straight weeks with any human, not even Gabe, not even my mother or father. For the first week I helped Sophie work on her first film, a 15-minute black and white vérité thing with a plot I couldn't follow, a plot she couldn't explain. During the second week we both decided I was a worthless production assistant, and we just lay on the beach together. After the third week we were done. It's not so much that we got sick of each other; it's more like our fantasy started sputtering and neither of us knew how to deal with the lack of full-throttle excitement.

Now, at my sunrise gate at LAX, she does cry as we say goodbye. A few tears even streak down her cheek and leave those salty trails. But there's something else there too, and I know I'm on my way out. Intuition is one crazy ghost.

(I will get my confirmation three weeks later in Prospect Park—the one in Providence—staring blankly at the puny skyline behind the statue of Roger Williams, wondering what just hit me even though I knew this was about to happen. That's the worst feeling in the world—when you know something's coming and it still shocks you. After she disses me on a park bench, she still tries to hold my hand through the perpetual Providence mist. Like a moron, I grab for her fingers. She walks me a few blocks down the lonely stretch of Benefit Street and then, as a parting gift, gives me the undisputed winner of the worst-hug-of-the-20th-century award.

On my last night in LA with her, she took me out to see the house I was born in, when Dad's music career was in full bloom, during the short kamikaze mission known as my parent's marriage, before we moved back East. The house was way out past Laurel Canyon. We came all the way from visiting her Aunt in Santa Barbara and there was traffic, so my birth house was harder to get to than either of us expected, and she wasn't even excited for me to see where I was born, more annoyed, almost blaming me for the distance, but I didn't know LA geography well.)

Too early in the morning at LAX, she is now looking at me with this glare. The glare says that she still doesn't know who she is, but she knows at the very least that whoever she is has nothing to do with me. That LAX look is the glare of futility. The look that says "Welcome to planet Earth, stranger. We hope you enjoyed your crash landing."

One year later that LAX look is fading from memory, and I don't even blame Sophie for it. All that is left clearly of her is that handicapped-bathroom-magic-mushroom stare. I bet the next time I run into her my smile will be magnificently doofy, and only 40% fake.

But to only keep the first memory, the magical one, doesn't seem real enough. I need both pictures to memorize Sophie in totality—the soft, the harsh—and if you don't keep your peeps properly and fully memorized, to what conclusion can experience come?

In *The Aleph*, after Jorge has seen and broken down the entire universe in a single ridiculous passage, he comes back to Beatriz.

That's how you know it's a love story. Whoever you give the last lines of your story, that's the one you really love. This is how *The Aleph* ends: "Our minds are porous with forgetfulness; I myself am falsifying and losing, through the tragic erosion of the years, the face of Beatriz."

[NOTE TO SELF: *After you've finished this insane writing spree, Alex, after you leave this Barcelona hostel, after you finish your program and leave Madrid and Spain, after you are back in los Estados Unidos, after you figure out why Gabe didn't come meet you here for your 21st birthday, after you know for sure if it's retaliation for you not being in London for his 22nd birthday, after you finally finish school, after the new millennium arrives and after the real world gets here, after you get settled into some bullshit routine or surrender to grad school, after you are a real adult with actual problems,* you need *to invent a time machine. You need to take this time machine on a journey to get an important question answered. Don't go back to the time of the Buddha; that'd be way too obvious, and way too far. The question you have is not a question for a guy like Siddhartha. This is a question for a guy like Jorge. Jorge died in 1986, and lived in Buenos Aires. You don't know much about the space-time continuum, but 1986 is probably, in terms of temporal mechanics, an easier trip backward than 560 BCE in India, anyway. And there's probably way less disease and way fewer snakes in mid 20th century Argentina. You are more like Jorge than the Buddha, anyway, Alex. Buddha wanted to know the universe and share it with* everyone. *That's not you, man. Jorge wanted to know the universe and share it with* somebody *special. Jorge is the one to ask what to do about people fading from memory like a shaken Etch-a-Sketch, about how to deal with losing Grandma and Sophie and Gabe. Whenever the real world comes for you and you have a real life and a real job and real problems, invent a time machine Alex, and find Jorge.*]

◆

Gabe comes back from the kitchen alone, and sees me slumped under the old gazebo for no apparent reason.

"Sophie?" He asks, his voice both gruff and telepathic. He scrunches up his face to light a cigarette.

"Yeah," I shrug. I tell him everything I am thinking as precisely as I can, because secrets have no market value between us.

"Yeah, I understand," he says. Then he says the most honest thing he's ever said to me in 13 years of friendship. "I've never even been in love." I know he's telling the truth. He's never even had a real girlfriend. Girls tend to think Gabe is amazing, until they have to sit through his first tirade.

"You just need a new lady, Al. How many girls have you gotten *nice* with since you and Sophie broke up?" he asks.

"I don't know. What do you mean 'gotten *nice* with'?" I wave off a few memories, set in the groping shadows of rooms I don't want to recall.

"Been with. Whatever."

"Nah, man." I shake him off again. "That's not anything. Anyway, compared to these motherfuckers," I gesture up to the general campgrounds, wherever Gideon and Anthony are scavenging for ladies at the moment, "it's nothing."

"Yeah, but who wants to be Gideon, you know?" He has a point. Being Gideon seems exhausting, to say the least. Gideon falls in love every four seconds. That must burn a ton of fossil fuel. "You're too smart for all those girls combined."

I take a breath and think about Gabe, about who he is to me, before speaking. "You're gonna find some philosophical, soft-edged girl in London who listens to your tirades and inspires 50 poems and that'll be the end of you, Little Moose." I laugh and slap him with an optimistic palm on the shoulder.

He shrugs again with the scrunched frown he always wears, lounging on the bench, the tip of his cigarette pointing a speck of mini-light out over the lake. I gotta give it up for Gabe, boy and girls. !!!!!!!!!!!!My Little Moose!!!!!!!!!!!!!! who sometimes thunders streamofgabe tirades like an autodidact preacher and other times sits calmly with me and meditates in dialogue, like now. He's my Little Moose either way, and that's why the name is perfect.

"Thanks for the vote of confidence, Al-Boogie," he says. "But you and I both know I won't be satisfied until I'm passed out in the London gutter with my pants around my ankles." We laugh. "Do they have Olde English forties in England?" he asks.

I think about it and say: "Yeah. But over there they just call them Olde forties." We laugh together at my bad joke, which Gabe thinks is hilarious. When Gabe thinks something is really funny, his body curls up into a ball with his hands convulsing back and forth. Now one hand flaps across his knees, the other hand trying to maintain control over his cigarette, to keep it from burning his stained blazer and Salvation Armani pants. He laughs and laughs, a volcano of phlegm.

"Do you think Happy'll bring me forties in London if I give him a big tip?"

"I don't know, man, he might deliver that far." I say.

◆

Happy is the owner and namesake of Happy's Village Deli and Grocery on 8th street. All summer long, they've delivered us our recommended daily allowance of malt liquor. Gideon figured out in a stroke of genius that it's possible to have forties delivered right to your apartment, a late May discovery that changed the course of the summer's history. Two other Pakistani guys, Sultan and Mike (Mike?) are Happy's delivery men. But Happy describes the entire enterprise, the whole exchange, and the name stuck. Gideon uses Happy as a verb, noun and adverb in conversation. As in, *Are we gonna Happy tonight? I need me some Happy. Happy Ever After, boys and girls. Pass me that cordless phone.* We've developed a system: $2.50 per forty, 50 cent tip per bottle; $3.00 each for door-to-door service (we usually order about five at a time, plus a pack of cigarettes, plus a couple of candy bars). We always invite Sultan and Mike to come in and drink with us when they bring the delivery, to try to get them to tell us something about their universe. But they never drink. Sometimes they'll smoke a cigarette with us on the balcony and watch the evening throngs passing under the Washington Square Arch across the street. I wish Happy were global, but he only delivers to a 10-block radius in the Village.

The parade of Happy summer nights was steady: standing out on Gideon's third floor balcony, people-watching and philosophizing in the early evening. The only hint of the real world was in the next morning's unpaid internship. After the right amount of social lubrication, we would either go out somewhere in the Village, or else stay in if there were enough people gathered at Gideon's to mark a party's critical mass, which there usually would be. (Gideon wields his cordless phone like a magic wand and an hour later interesting characters just ring his doorbell, arriving from all corners of the City.) Either way we'd eventually crash like bums in his empty apartment because his entire family was gone for the summer. I could always stumble home the 10 blocks to Dad's apartment, but I preferred to go fetal-position in the perfect cradle of the hammock on Gideon's balcony, listening to the wind rustling Washington Square. On weeknights, we would all hear Gideon yelling "This is wack!" three times at 7:00am the next morning, in response to his alarm clock. When I heard him yell "this is wack" the third time, 10 minutes after the initial buzz, that was my signal that I had to wake up too. Gideon's yell was my snooze button. We rose and crawled upright to summer jobs and internships.

◆

Gabe and I walk up to the camp's kitchen to get more beers. We nod to Santa Claus, who nods back politely. Inside, Gideon, Anthony, Lucas, and London Denise are talking in loud voices.

"What the hell are you talking about?" Gideon says to

London Denise. His voice sounds rambunctious, at the peak of drunkenness. "That girl *loved* me. She gave me her digits." He holds up a crumpled sheet of looseleaf with a number on it as evidence.

"You can't just barge in on people like that while they're sleeping, you know," Denise protests.

"Oh, They *LOVED* it," Gideon says, then turns and sees me. "What up Alex? We missed you. We thought you were in some kind of trance down there." He hands me a thick stack of about 50 American Cheese slices from the massive fridge without saying why. I pop one in my mouth. Gideon tells me they snuck into the cottage where the laundresses and garbage girls and head cook all live, and woke them all up just to have someone new to talk to. One of the garbage girls was from Jersey, and he shook her shoulders until she opened her eyes to see him hovering above her. "At first she was kinda scared and confused," he says, "but it turned into a good conversation and I got her number. But then *London* came," he motions angrily at Denise, "and practically dragged us out of there." He folds three slices of American Cheese into his mouth. "Why the hell is she still chilling with us anyway?" He spits on the floor.

"Hey *London*," Gideon calls over to her.

"What?" she says, sounding irritated.

"Who's the best looking of all of us?"

She doesn't answer. Gideon asks again. "I said, who's the best looking of all of us?"

"I think it's a tie." She nervously points to Anthony and me. This surprises me. Anthony has these amazing blue eyes, alive like ecosystems. My mother—all our mothers—used to talk about his eyes when we were in eighth grade, which made me more than a bit uncomfortable. If Anthony could find a girl from this continent who he liked enough, he'd be in business. But he's off to Dublin in a few weeks anyway for the year, so maybe it's a good omen that all these foreign girls are sweating him. Gideon is a little aggravated that "London," with her too-round face and bad short haircut, wants Anthony, because according to Gabe they have this nature-channel competition about girls that dates back to being 16 and racing each other to lose their virginities. Everything goes back to high school and nature-channels in the end.

"Alright," Gideon says, probing. "Anthony and Alex, tied for first. I don't mind that at all. They've both had a ton of work done on their faces, just so you know, though." Anthony hurls a balled-up cheese slice at Gideon's head. "So, am I third?" No answer. London Denise squirms, shy. "I won't get offended, believe me sweetheart. I just wanna know where I stand."

She recognizes the trap. "No, I won't rank you, you know," she waves him off.

"Sweetheart, you're overestimating how much you can affect me with your answer."

"Don't call me sweetheart," she says.

"*Honey,*" Gideon corrects himself, putting on a charm he genuinely doesn't know is condescending, "I just wanna be informed. Okay, so I'm not first or second. Am I third?"

Silence.

"Fourth?"

Uncomfortable silence.

"Fifth?"

Denise is looking nervously at the floor.

"Sixth?"

No answer. Then Gideon gets up in her face because she's avoiding eye contact like a pro. He shouts at the top of his lungs: "THERE'S ONLY FIVE OF US!"

We all burst out laughing—even Gabe—but London Denise looks visibly scared now. Gideon thankfully backs off. "Don't worry, you don't have to tell me." He picks the tall pile of cheese slices up off the table. With a drunken southpaw windup, he hurls them at the wall. They stick for an anticlimactic fraction of a second before sliding down to the floor.

"Let's roll back to the bunk," Anthony says, touching Gideon mercifully on the shoulder. We each grab another beer. London Denise follows us down the trail and into our bunk. We all get into our beds, and she climbs into the one remaining empty bunk bed and lies down.

It's pretty obvious that she's completely smitten with Anthony, who is already faking sleep. Given that I'm her second choice, I pretend to pass out, too. Gideon and Lucas are beyond drunk and want to keep messing around, so they go over to her bunk and climb in. Lucas starts kissing Denise's neck and Gideon starts rubbing her thick legs. She's laughing by now, having figured out that they're harmless, letting herself be amused by the affection. I go into the bathroom to brush my teeth, figuring it's safe now that she's distracted. But she eventually pushes them off of her, and when I come back from the sink she's alone in the bed. Lucas is lying on top of Gideon, an awkward embrace on the dirty bunk floor. Eventually Denise realizes Anthony won't be joining her and she leaves, her fantasy squashed.

"Ant," Gideon lifts his head and whisper-yells through the darkness. "Anthony!"

"What?" Anthony answers, irritated and wide-awake.

"You're a fuckin' asshole."

"Why?"

"Cause all London wanted in the world was for you to get with her, and you couldn't even grant her one simple wish." Gideon suddenly sounds deeply sad and compassionate, even charitable.

"Why didn't *you* get nice with her, then?" Anthony argues.

"Why? CAUSE I WAS FUCKIN' SIXTH OUT OF FIVE!" Gideon shouts.

"Shut up," Lucas says, slapping Gideon hard in the face on the floor. "People are sleeping."

"My bad," Gideon says. "Ant, you could've made her day. That's all I'm gonna say. Fuck—6th out of 5," he says again, unbelieving.

I pass out. In the only dream I half-remember, Grandma is feeding me Macadamia Brittle ice cream in the backyard of her country house. She spoon-feeds it to me with a huge wooden ladle from an outdoor bathtub filled with Häagen-Daz.

THE LAKE AFTER THE STORM

I WAKE UP AND WIPE A TEAR from my crusty eye, adjusting back to this planet. Lucas wants to go water-skiing, and I realize there's still a little more playtime left.

We set out across the massive lake in Camp's newest ski boat, with Lucas behind the steering wheel. The day is partly cloudy, more humid than the last two. Anthony predicts a storm later, in that quiet Traveling Man voice that makes you assume he must be right. The motor churns the dark water into froth behind us, until it dissolves back into the lake without a trace. I can't ski because my ankle is still swollen. When Gabe's shaggy head lifts above the spew of churning water created by his submerged body, we don't know if he'll make it upright. I root for him silently and his feet break the plane. He starts gliding, polishing the lake's mirror, adept and balanced. We all cheer. But then Lucas starts taking the ski boat on crazy turns and diabolical jolts and eventually Gabe lets go of the line.

Gideon decides to ski without his bathing suit. We all laugh hysterically as the motor revs, and when he snaps up, conquering the watery plane, there's little Giddy, still stubbly from his porn-star shave, hanging out from under the bottom of the yellow lifejacket. We pass other boats and all wave to them, including Gideon. They may be too far away to fully, um, grasp, um, little Giddy.

[NOTE TO SELF: *You do realize, Alex, since you are the witty coward, that Gideon's summer courage was probably assisted by lines of white powder. More than once in his apartment and at bars you saw him disappear into the bathroom at strange moments with shady characters. But that's not the optimistic thing to believe. It's better for a witty coward to believe that all outrageous behavior is fueled by something more untouchably organic.*]

After Gideon is done skiing, the boat idles in the middle of the vast gray-blue lake-scape. I throw myself over the railing and let the water take all the mugginess off my skin.

We dock at a gas station for boats way across the lake. I marvel aloud at the fact that boats have their own gas stations, but nobody else thinks it's that interesting an observation. We let the attendant fill up the tank as we walk across the road, the hot August cement baking our bare feet—to a take-out ice cream and fried clams stand (I have no idea who threw those two foods together, especially next to a lake full of choppy waters). The girl who works the stand looks about our age. Gideon is instantly all over her. She is extremely cute, with big eyes, short blond hair, tight white shorts, and a gray UVM tee shirt. A bell at the counter has a little sign that says "Ring for Service." Every time she tries to take two steps from the counter to fill our order, Gideon taps the bell so she won't go. She's polite and playful about it for a while, but Gideon doesn't know when to stop.

She finally tells Gideon, to get him to leave, that she's only a senior in high school and she has a boyfriend. I picture her boyfriend as a non-descript varsity athlete who she's been going out with since freshman year. Gideon tells her to come join us at the outdoor picnic table in the grass if she gets a break. She says "sure" but never comes. We eat our fried clams and milkshakes, which we put on the camp's tab again, and get back in the boat.

Right after we dock back at camp, a torrential downpour starts.

"Told ya," Anthony says in his confident Traveling Man voice. I'm feeling a little upset now, as the rain starts to shake branches and pelt the earth.

"Fellas, Homies, Players, Comrades," I say, in a moment of inspired leadership, "Promise we won't let anything stop playtime

---

70

until it's time to leave Camp."

"Word up," Anthony says, wrapping his arm around my back and rubbing my head under the temporary shelter of a tree. We go to the indoor rec center, which campers nicknamed the "Putter-Dome", after Lucas' family. We play five-on-five full court basketball against the last of the remaining counselors. The power goes out because of the storm, so we open the huge barn-like sliding door on one side of the court to let some light in, though it isn't much. It's tough to shoot for a while, and Gabe falls flat on his face running in the dark, but we aren't about to stop—we have taken a solemn vow to play. I'm still hobbling, even though the swelling has gone down, and I can't bang around inside, even though I'm the second tallest player on our team behind Lucas. Lucas throws his belly around in dark shadows under the rim, and Anthony, both the strongest and best athlete among us, clears room under the boards. I start knocking down some outside shots, seeing through the darkness somehow, and manage to make my contribution despite my certified gimp status. We lose a few close games though, because a few of the counselors have serious skills, and we can't coordinate as a team. Eventually, Anthony and Lucas start blaming each other for not boxing out. Then Lucas starts yelling at Gabe for not getting back on defense fast enough, but Gabe can't help it—my man's a poet with nicotine lungs and bad eyesight. I tell Lucas to chill and leave Gabe alone, and now everybody's fighting each other, eradicating what little team chemistry we might've had.

After the downpour the power comes back on but the running water doesn't, so we can't shower. I take a towel and a bar of soap and head off alone, gimping a long way down the shore, maybe even off Camp property. Nobody notices my absence. I almost kill myself climbing down into the water over the tree roots and slippery rocks. When my head surfaces from a half-accidental dunking, the whole lake is suddenly vibrant, in a dull blue-gray kinda way. The water is cooler now, revived after the storm. The unruffled color is surrounded on all edges by trees, except in the distance where the lake opens into a much larger pocket. It feels like the Lake is an event outside time's reach, a true *moment*, not just a future memory. I wish Dad were here, because he has that spacious Taoist nature that appreciates these things.

I decide here and now that the first thing I will do when I get back to the City on Thursday, in the tiny window of time left before I leave again, will be to find Dad, wherever he is, and apologize. He might also owe me an apology, but that's ok. Grandma might owe us both a huge apology, and my Great-grandparents might owe her an even bigger apology, and all the way down the family tree there might be exponentially bigger and bigger sorrys due, as we trace the generations back toward the dawn of civilization, and the very first single-celled organism might owe a big fat intergalactic "my bad" to every sentient being that came after, but none of that has to do with me finding Dad.

◆

Last week, before this road trip began, the Wannabe Poet's Brigade had a rare evening meeting on a stoop. I picked up the cordless phone on Gideon's balcony and called Gabe at his parents' new condo in Westchester. I was upset about the afternoon's therapy session and more upset that I had to dial 914 if I wanted to reach Gabe at home now, pissed at his parents for selling out and leaving the Village behind them as soon as their nest was empty. I told Gabe to get his ass on the Metro-North quickfast, and bring me some good words.

Our meeting started with Happy. Surprise. Not only does Happy deliver to Gideon's apartment, he facilitates the ability to drink on stoops. Gabe and I had a new foolproof plan for public consumption, which in the age of Giuliani is an increasingly dangerous pastime. We figured out that malt liquor is precisely the same urinal hue as Arizona green iced tea, so we collected four empty 20-ounce bottles of tea in Gabe's bag. We each bought a forty, and Sultan let Gabe behind the sandwich counter to pour the malt liquor carefully into the tea bottles. No extra charge, Sultan said, though we tipped him a dollar in the sandwich tip jar. Problem solved. Happy was our summertime MVP, our perpetual Village All-Star.

On a stoop down the block from Cooper Union, we started sharing words. I read a short love poem, an after-love poem, actually. I could tell Gabe wasn't feeling it at all. Gabe has these three different frowns. Frown #1 says "I'm thinking about something really hard." That's actually the most obvious frown, and that's how you know there's a 70-75% chance of a streamofgabe tirade coming soon. Frown #2 is the most often used frown. It says, "I disagree with what just happened", which is almost a frown/smile combo, eyes scrunched. Frown #2 can also be used to note an injustice, either on a personal or global scale. Frown #3 is the subtlest, with the least facial muscle involvement, and it represents severe aesthetic displeasure in Gabe's entire being. Frown #3 is the most devastating. After I read my poem, Gabe didn't say anything, but just frowned Frown #3. That put me in a defensive mood.

Then Gabe read a poem called "war and pieces," which I thought was way too long and preachy. I felt deflated. I got that achey feeling you get when the exhibition doesn't go well, that feeling that says you may as well never express anything again, because all the expressions are going to be obsolete before they even make it out of your mind and into shared reality. I hate that overly sensitive feeling. It tells me I should just use the rest of Grandma's inheritance to go to law school, get comfortable, and stop wasting everyone's time.

We pause the poetry for a while, a little disgusted with ourselves and each other.

[NOTE TO SELF: *When you get back to los Estados Unidos, remember you must write a more formal obituary for the August 1998 passing of the Wannabe Poets Brigade, a death by natural causes.*]

Gabe sipped malt liquor from the iced tea bottle and started talking about my Dad, telling me he'd been listening to his lyrics, asking me if I'd ever really listened to them because they were simple and funny and deep. Gabe said "Your Dad's a great artist." I have all Dad's lyrics memorized, at least the '70s stuff, but I didn't want to talk folk music. Instead I started spilling my guts about my therapist, about what she'd been saying for weeks, what she said earlier in the day.

She said that our time together for now, for the summer, was almost done, and that I should finally confront my father before I went away. She had high hopes that this year would be powerful and transformative for me, and if it started off with clarity, that could only be helpful. Gabe just listened for a long time, listened to me list all the reasons I didn't need to bother Dad, saying that nothing was anybody's fault, really, that our drama was nothing special compared to most dramas, that everybody always tries their best, etc, blah blah blah.

Finally Gabe just said, very quietly, "That's retarded." It caught me off guard. The thing about Gabe is this: he's *très* annoying, for sure, but he's not an offensive kid. He's actually deceptively polite when any parents or professors are around.

The word *retarded* actually means something important, even when it doesn't refer to disabled people. It means your way of thinking is stuck, drowning in quicksand. Gabe uses the word *retarded* sometimes, but he's careful never to say it about people. He only says it about ideas and concepts, and only when he thinks they've gotten hopelessly stuck in some kind of spasm. The way those two words came out of his mouth, in something just louder than a whisper, convinced me to go find Dad.

I stumbled down the block to find a pay phone and crouched into the new Bell Atlantic booth, pulling a lint-covered quarter out of my jeans.

"Of course, I'm here, come on over," Dad said, excited to hear my voice, oblivious to his coming ambush. I took off down Bowery without saying peace to Gabe, abandoned on the stoop with malt liquor backwash in an Arizona iced tea bottle, futon-less, carelessly disregarded by the worst best friend in history.

Rounding the corner onto Prince, I could feel the pull to turn around, to retrace my steps and leave it for another night. I went to the roof to clear my head. Dad's roof is my shrine. Unfortunately, since Sophie dissed me, I spent a lot of my time there staring off toward California in the continental expanse, pretending this strange planet was flatter and bite-size, imagining my 310-Sophie and her 415-new-boyfriend in San Francisco, triangulating their two auras like I had satellite software in my brain.

If I wasn't thinking of Sophie on the roof, my many hours on the soft tar were spent contemplating what I was going to do whenever the real world arrived. In no particular order, I hoped it would be one of three things: I'd either A) become a famous wannabe-writer (not superfamous, just quasi-underground-famous); B) do something as-yet-undefined to help out a few strange earthlings in some small (but obviously noteworthy) way; or C) disappear into a Himalayan cave and meditate until only hair and fingernails remain, printing my verses on sheets of rainbow light. My main dilemma was that the schmancy education gifted to me by Grandma's death seemed in service of exactly none of these three options, so I was perpetually selling out on her legacy. A lot of guilty thoughts polluted the air above Dad's soft-tar roof at the foot of Prince Street, thicker than any Manhattan smoke stack.

I tried to clear my head by following my breath, but instead I followed my drunk, and felt the sticky August air clinging to my white tee. Eventually I climbed down the stairwell and felt for the right key on my crowded keychain. The door creaked open into the loft, and I saw the wall of music photos that adorned the entryway, all the famous people Dad had played with over the years.

Dad sat on the couch, passive and thoughtful, stroking his face. I perched on the Ottoman that used to be in Grandma's apartment uptown, now orphaned here. He offered me a beer and I accepted. When he came back from the refrigerator, I looked up behind him at the Grammy statue on the piano, next to a picture of Dad's new girlfriend. (When Amelia asked me why I don't like Dad's new lady, my only response had nothing to do with her; instead I said the problem was that prime photographic real estate ought to be toiled for and earned, and this woman hadn't been on the scene nearly long enough to deserve the best plot of photographic terrain in the loft, the piano; seriously, even Dad's siblings were visually relegated to the bookshelf in the corner.) The Grammy statue made me laugh. Once in June — when Dad was away and the party was here for the night — Gideon successfully convinced a girl the Grammy was his own. She didn't inspect it closely before following him into my old bedroom-turned-office, or she would've realized it was from 1976, and the self-proclaimed winner of "Best New Artist" was much older than he looked.

I sipped the beer and said I wanted to talk. Dad said, "I thought we already were talking." Awkwardness ensued. After a silence, I stumbled through family mythologies, kamikaze marriages, unfinished accusations, unresolveable arguments, unanswerable questions, accidental deaths and more accidental births, until finally the meanest and half-truest thing I could say came through my lips, clear as a bell.

"You're the whole reason I never had family, just random relatives." It felt like I was firing a water gun filled with bleach, aiming for Dad's chin.

After a long pause, he shook his head slowly and said, "I understand." No defense, no apology. Just *I understand*. What the fuck is *understand?* That's not even a thing!

I stopped talking. Everything I might say felt profoundly retarded. Instead, I decided to let out a few semi-automatic rounds of angry thought.

Fuck the motherfucking dharma.
And Double-fuck you Dad, for not being enlightened.
And Triple-Fuck Me, for not even being able to handle this wack cliché called heartbreak.

I wanted to leave. But nobody was waiting for me to be anywhere else, and if nobody's waiting for you anywhere, then wanting to leave just makes you feel exponentially worse. I made myself stay. Dad started talking again eventually, and then I joined him in chit-chat and we were churning voices, small talk and big talk building, discussing stupid things and crucial things all wrapped up into one sushi roll called dialogue. A few hours later, I didn't feel so on fire anymore. Dad lightened up too, and he must've felt more comfortable about talking, because he took me into family histories, way into them, way more than he had ever shared before.

Dad opened a new doorway onto my inheritance. The fact is that suicide weaves itself all through our family history, like a missing thread. This fact wasn't new, even if it had never been addressed directly. I think that's why Dad got into Buddhism, to find someway to deal with all the nihilism stockpiled in his genes. Not me, though. I got into Buddhism to impress an art school chick.

Sometime after midnight, he told me about Grandma. He said that her death two years ago was also a suicide, some morphine arrangement to avoid the painful degeneration of her cancer. I remembered how quickly she'd gone after the diagnosis, after that Spring night in the taxi crossing Central Park when she just said "my back hurts" and decided to make a doctor's appointment. But that wasn't all Dad told me. His whole adult life had been an exercise in watching his mother's constant dance with depression, and her constant threats to end it. Her first real attempt happened on his 19th birthday. He got the phone call when he was lying in bed, naked with his own Sophie. In all, there were three suicide attempts, one half-hearted, two serious, both of which should've killed Grandma long before I crash-landed onto Earth and into the Matriarchy of her world.

I never knew Grandma that way at all, it had all stayed hidden to me, but I could tell Dad wasn't exaggerating her darkness. If anything, he was probably still downplaying everything, because that's his style.

There are the things you keep in mind to list, the important things about the important people. You keep them bulletpointed, like some dossier, so if anybody ever asks why they're so important you can tell them quickly:

- Grandma was a feminist before there was a word for it, she told me when I was reading Steinem in her country house.

- She was a successful creative woman before it was legal to be one.

- She was the first grown-up to talk to me like I was a grown-up too, and she started doing that when I was about four years old.

- She took me to Tae Kwon Do class and Broadway plays.

- She read every last sentence I ever wrote and has been paying me for my poetry since I was 12 years old.

- She told me randomly when I was 13 that it would be totally fine if I were gay, which somehow I managed not to take the wrong way at all.

- She kept her country house freezer stocked with 20 pints of ice cream, and her City apartment stocked with 10 pints on the off chance I would want some.

- She always let me stay with her as long as I wanted.

Most of the time, given all my options, I wanted to stay with Grandma a mighty long time.

I looked up at the microwave clock. It read 12:45am. Dad's voice came at me ethereally, through a swirl of dizziness. "You were her bright spot, Alex. Her biggest bright spot." I looked back at him and tried to focus my eyes, but nothing would let them stick. I finally focused on the eyebrows he was raising at me. My dad has an intense stare, especially when he raises those thick brows. I started crying. Not wailing, just crying softly. It lasted a while. Then I was done.

We kept talking. I raided the fridge for another beer, a beer he said I didn't need, a sentence I pretended not to hear. I remember the last thing I said was some streamofgabe diatribe about nihilism and postmodernism and chemical depression, which had nothing to do with anything I was feeling, as per usual. I woke up on the couch. Dad had tucked me under a light blanket and put my favorite pillow under my head. I felt the blast of the air conditioner coating my shoulders. The sun was piercing from behind the restaurant supply store on Bowery, and Brooklyn and Europe behind that. It was five minutes before I had to leave to get to my internship on time. The smell of Japanese incense was coming from Dad's half-open bedroom door, so I grabbed aspirin for the day and left without a goodbye.

When it's time to pull my body out of Lake Winnipesaukee, I almost kill myself again. I sit on a tree stump and try to meditate with my gimpy ankle extended in front of me. Sophie comes to mind, with her mushroom-bathroom-floor stare, but the memory now is like a little cloud puffing in the August sky.

Suddenly, I start giggling. The giggle grows, then grows more, and finally I'm laughing so hard I almost fall off the stump. I really wish I knew why I lost it; truly uncontrollable laughter would be a good thing to be able to reproduce on command. I can't stop; there's a seismic event happening in my gut. I don't know if you ever had one of those moments where existence is a beautiful, but sorta cheesy knock-knock joke, and the punchline is *you*. It goes on for about 10 minutes on that tree stump, laughter and laughter, without subject or object. And when the eruption subsides, a thought comes to me: *I think I might be actually starting to like myself.* Walking back to the bunk, I feel all cold and cozy, shivering with goosebumps and limping in the dirt.

THE FORTUNE COOKIE

TOWARDS DINNER TIME, CARL KNOCKS ON THE bunk door and offers to take us on a long ride in the ski boat. It's our last night at camp, after all, he says. As the motor revs up, I can feel summer dying. We go farther across the lake than I've ever been, all the way to Wolfeboro. Carl's voice sounds like a tour guide, displaying the huge houses along the shifting waterfront, speaking loudly over the roaring motor and backrushing air. Lucas looks completely disinterested by his father, resisting every verbal invitation Carl throws his way, which makes me feel awful. It's their last night together, too. This time next week Lucas will be in Madison, Wisconsin, and Carl will be on the road again, searching for parents to send him their boys next summer, trying to rustle up some more playtime-capital.

Why are we so brutal to each other?

A lightning storm develops just as we get back to Camp, and we make it just in time. I can see individual lightning bolts not too far away in the ripening darkness, and I wish I knew more about electricity, the exact forces that draw neon cracks in the marbled sky.

We say goodnight to Carl and pile in the Range Rover. The windshield wipers are sleek and silent through this new storm. We drive to a nearby Chinese restaurant. City kids usually regard rural Chinese restaurants with appropriate suspicion, but this place has major sentimental value for Lucas and Anthony. Counselors used to come here to buy late night feasts for their campers, collecting money up front and charging a high delivery premium, which campers were happy to pay to get something other than camp food. The name of the restaurant, "The Fortune Cookie," is different, but inside it looks exactly the same.

Gabe quickly falls in love with the waitress. His heart is random but utterly specific, no loveslut like Gideon. She just started working there, and has a southern hospitality the management of the place lacks. She's the only non-Chinese person on staff. From what she says, they aren't all that good to her. We ask about the large flaming drinks at the next table. In her subtle Texan drawl, she tells us which ones and how many we should get in order to "knock us on our ass." She's about 30, with long blond hair and a nondescript figure. Her energy is steady and kind, without any flash. She just moved to the middle of New Hampshire from Houston, to be with her fella, and she shows us her wedding ring. She talks about some of the interesting people she met at a Harley-Davidson convention a few weeks ago. That's right about when Gabe falls in love with her.

Our feast is greasy and endless. We're not even sure what we're celebrating, but Lucas, our playtime patron, insists that we are celebrating something, and keeps ordering for us. The table is full of flaming drinks and garlic sauces. The drinks don't knock me on my ass as promised, but it's not the waitress' fault. My tolerance is crazily high at summer's end.

She makes numerous visits to check on us and chat. It's late on a stormy Monday and we outlast all the other tables, but she doesn't ask us to leave in any hurry. Gabe tells her that she's the best waitress he's ever had. His voice has the humble sincerity of a marriage proposal. She gets flustered. When she recovers, she tells him he's sweet. He shrugs it off and goes back to being a gruff Little Moose. We leave a huge tip, almost 50%, after she writes on the back of our check in bubbly handwriting: "You guys were the best customers I've had since I got here. Get wherever you're headed safe and sound — Joyce."

As the namesake of the restaurant, the fortune cookies are sub-par. They're stale, and mine says something to the effect of "you're a really good person", only a little more cryptic than that. That's not even a fortune. A fortune tells you your goddamn future.

We stand around in the parking lot for a while. It stopped raining, and I smoke a cigarette with Gabe. Anthony comes out after going to the bathroom, and says, with quiet Traveling Man swagger: "The waitress told me to say good-bye again. And she also said we were the most interesting group of young men she'd seen in a long time."

"She's wonderful," Gabe says, beaming.

For the millionth time, I try to imagine the kind of lady who will someday make Gabe feel possessive and pursue her, but I can't figure it out. It's possible he's gay, but more likely he's just not that sexual. He might be right; he'll end up in the London gutter with his pants around his ankles, indifferent. But in that case, I hope he'll have some writing in his pocket (like the day at the beginning of summer, when things felt new and pregnant and possible after we all saw Damien perform at Nuyoricans Poets Café, when I came home from the first day of my magazine internship and found Gabe sitting on the loading dock next to Dad's building, waiting for me to get back home so he'd have somewhere-anywhere to be, smoking and scribbling), writing that would "knock you on your ass."

We head back to Camp, find more beer, and head into the lodge. We play ping-pong and get beat senseless at foosball by the same counselors who beat us at basketball earlier in the Putter-Dome. We are, apparently, good for the counselors' self-esteem. One dude has an Olympic level foosball talent, a skill that will definitely carry him far in life. The laundresses and the garbage girls are here too, drinking more boxed wine, but they're uninterested in us, as if last night never happened.

RANDOM ITHACA

EARLY IN THE MORNING, CARL FEEDS US bagels and we say peace to Lucas.

"Thanks for the playtime," I say, and hug him, more strongly than I usually hug one of my boys. Maybe I'll see him at Thanksgiving, maybe not. It's not like that between us, and it never was. This trip was an accident and we both know it.

We're off driving again, with Gabe behind the wheel of the black Mazda, me navigating in shotgun, Gideon and Anthony in the back seat. I get the navigating job because I'm good at problem solving. I figure this is possibly the first time in history that anyone has driven from this tiny spot in New Hampshire directly to Ithaca, NY.

"Ithaca is just fuckin' *random*," Gabe says, when he hears the complexity of the route I propose. We decide that henceforth the town will be officially renamed Random Ithaca. On Alex Bardo's Famously Bad Mix Tape #3, Otis is preaching about being Chained and Bound. We work our way through the 30 minutes of local roads back to the highway. In Concord we start heading west. Voices go silent and we listen to music and tires and the hum of air. The road winds west as I trace the Northeast beneath my long fingers on Gabe's map. The map is wide, thin, and delicate, constantly ripping at the center crease, no matter how much I try to be still and preserve it. It will rip in half somewhere in the middle of upstate New York, when I don't need it anymore.

Somewhere within the overwhelming quaintness of Green Mountain National Forest, we stop to buy cigarettes. "Alex," Anthony says, as Gabe pulls us out of the country store parking lot.

"Yeah," I respond.

"You've studied Marx a lot, right, and his critiques of capitalism?" Anthony is majoring in Sociology and Peace & Justice studies, the perfect Traveling Man Double Major.

"Yeah, man. It's pretty unavoidable." I shrug.

"I'd like to hear your thoughts on it," he says, leaning forward behind me.

"At this moment I like capitalism better," I say simply.

"Why?" he asks, surprised (I often had the 2nd edition Marx-Engels reader with me on Gideon's balcony).

My first answer was spontaneous, and now I have to think for a minute.

"Capitalism has better camps and better road trips. But you have to love people on the trip, which Capitalism doesn't really teach you how to do. Otherwise road trips are pointless."

Anthony nods slowly in the rearview, his gorgeous eyes uncertain. Neither one of us understands me, but we talk about it for a little while anyway. The road is hilly and dense with tall trees all around—a beautiful stretch—and I let my mind cascade outward to meet the nature rushing back toward us. Gray marshmallow clouds near, and we're all a little nervous about Gabe's driving abilities in inclement weather, but it only sprouts a puny drizzle that stops soon after crossing into New York State. We keep talking about Economics and Sociology and Modern Culture and Media and English and Art and Society and how it's all good and all the same thing anyway, which is the politically correct way to end a conversation whenever your brain hurts from running itself in circles.

"Why aren't you doing any creative writing at school?" Gabe asks me.

I get surprisingly defensive and slap him on the shoulder. "I'm doin' a ton of writing up there. That's all I do, man; you know that. That's where I started my book." I am at work on a first volume of Wannabe Poetry in my spare time, which might not be finished for many years. More accurately, it's a monstrous cloud of words, because *volume* implies some nonexistent purpose of publication. "I do that instead of all my homework."

"I mean *structured* writing. With guidance. You should try to take more actual writing classes." Gabe is an English major, a fact that I find *très* annoying. I don't want to take any more writing classes. I took a writing class last year. I wasn't feeling it. It felt remedial, inherently patronizing, the way that someone telling you how to play feels patronizing. If I write like *playtime,* it isn't work, and if it isn't work, I'm approximately 900% more likely to do it.

It wasn't work this summer. I'd wake up in Gideon's hammock on the balcony, roll to my internship, go to one of my parents' apartments and change, pretend to meditate, write for a few hours, take a nap, head back to Gideon's apartment, get back in the hammock, and summon Happy's Village Deli on Gideon's cordless phone.

"You gotta read the classics," Gabe says to me now, in defense of academia.

"I am reading the classics," I say. "I'm just not depending on them."

I launch into a Gabe-esque diatribe that Gabe has already heard before, about a survey course on Shakespeare that Sophie convinced me to take, and how it was the worst class I've ever taken at any level of my schmancy education. I don't think Shakespeare is all that great, by the way. Sorry, I know that's illegal to even say. Hear me out. I honestly believe he may have led the literary traditions of Earth down a path where you aren't allowed to express emotions directly and just say how you actually *feel.* What if his style of storytelling helped doom Western Society to a 500-act play of narrative melodrama and true emotional repression? Did you ever consider that possibility? That maybe the way we tell stories is the reason we can't express our feelings on this strange planet? I know this is an extreme view...

but it's a valid view, except it's the one view you aren't allowed to hold in a $4,000 course on Shakespeare, and that's the entire problem with academia—all views are definitely *not* on the table. And if all views are not on the table, if even one possible view remains unconsidered, then you can't really call it learning. Sometimes this planet and its strange ideas just get me a little heated.

I argue with Gabe for a little while more about Willie, wanting to blow my brains out, but thankfully Anthony interrupts from shotgun without segue, suddenly talking in his quiet voice about how much he wants to visit Machu Picchu and study shamanism. We stop for gas, Anthony takes over driving and we catch the massive interstate. The Captain America shields return to the road. The conveyor belt moves us West, faster than before, so fast it feels like time is warping Star Trek-style, except the warping stars are all warping trees and warping lane-dashes. I'm in the back seat now with Gideon, and Gabe grabs shotgun. No fan of mix tapes (he considers them an insult to the intentions of the original albums the songs came from), he throws in Bob Dylan's *Highway 61 Revisited* and starts shouting the words:

He starts air-drumming or seat-dancing or something, his body soon becoming insanely convulsive, like when he was laughing uncontrollably in the gazebo. Suddenly Gabe's turning shotgun into his own private mosh pit, which is a hard thing to do to a song that's not very fast-paced and features a party-favor whistle. Gideon starts laughing at him, but Gabe doesn't notice, violently shaking the back of his seat into my cramped knees with his Dylan-slam-dance, screaming altered lines like: *GABE SAID 'WHERE YOU WANT THIS KILLING DONE?' GOD SAID 'ON HIGHWAY 61!'*

And then a few minutes later, when Gabe settles down, suddenly silent in his seat, I hear my favorite song, Just Like Tom Thumb's Blues. After Sophie dissed me, I pretty much burned a hole in the CD listening to that song. *"I'M GOIN' BACK*

TO NEW YORK CITY," I sing now, trying to recapture the old musical voice that my puberty wrecked, *"I DO BELIEVE I'VE HAD ENNNNOOOOUUUGGGGHHH."*

◆

As the Black Mazda gets closer to Random Ithaca, Gideon's face darkens, more serious than I've seen it anytime over the summer.

"Yo, all joking aside, when we get to my apartment, I want ZERO discussion of my activities this summer. Diana doesn't need to know." We all laugh.

Diana is Gideon's girlfriend. Yes, he actually has a committed girlfriend. Tonight, we are delivering Gideon to her in Random Ithaca, to a real shared apartment and everything. He's the first kid I know my own age who is going to live with someone and make an actual nest. According to Gideon, Diana has some vague idea of his unique brand of scumbaggedness (insofar as it's part of his charm), but not much. She's from Arizona, or some other state I can't remember, mythically far from NYC. He slept with eight or nine other women this summer (depending on who's doing the counting, one of whom was a newly-divorced 43-year-old friend of Anthony's mom — another story for another time). When he told me about Diana, I was shocked he had a girlfriend, but I could tell that he loved her, and I'll testify it to her face if she ever finds out about his summer.

He just doesn't see much future with her, I guess. He said she'll meet someone else as soon as he leaves to study in Prague this January, and he wants to get a Czech girlfriend when he's there because he thinks that'll be the only way he'll learn a new language. He actually thinks that way, no joke.

He falls in love with girls all the time for the strangest reasons. He fell in love with a girl he'd never see again at a hot dog stand in Toronto because of the lack of hesitation and ease with which she said the word "vagina." He fell in love with a girl from New Jersey just because she didn't call him back for a month. I bet he actually fell in love with London Denise after she refused to rank him. The weird thing about it is how real his declarations of love seem, at least when he makes them in his six-year-old voice. He says he wants to hold onto Diana for as long as he can, and that means we have to shut up in her presence, preserve the illusion of his nest. That's what he said to me about her, as I lay cradled in the hammock by Washington Square. "She's my nest, or some bullshit."

Anthony has his Hong Kong lady up here too, the hotel heiress. I remember that Amelia is here too, the closest thing to a lady I have right now. Even if it's just a lady of that excruciating best-friend variety, even if she's currently visiting her boyfriend up in Random Ithaca, I am looking forward to wrapping my arms around a feminine presence who knows me well, someone who doesn't have all this ludicrous testosterone bumrushing her being.

We get to Random Ithaca around 6:30pm. Gideon pulls out the keys to his new apartment in a split-level house. Diana isn't home yet. I feel deep excitement for him. The place has a remodeled kitchen his girlfriend plans to steam a lot of kale in, a cozy little living room, and an open porch that spans the front face of the split house. Gabe and I do laundry, washing every thing we have with us, except for boxers and Gabe's blazer, which he insists should be dry-cleaned (hypothetical dry cleaning is apparently better care than actual washing). We sit on the porch almost naked, un-self-conscious. Gabe's brown nipples poke out from the lapels of his blazer. We watch back-to-school pedestrians streaming down the busy College-town street.

Later we sit on the porch, diving into forties and whiskey and the evening air of a new locale. The back-to-school vibe on the street is palpable, and I feel one part excitement and two parts horror swirling in me like a lopsided yin and yang. Anthony steps onto the porch wearing his slightly imperfect wifebeater, his muscles rippling without sleeves to hide them. This inspires the rest of us to go get on our slightly imperfect wifebeaters, as if they are our team uniform. Diana comes home, and I give her a hug and a sloppy kiss on the cheek, as if we've been tight since the sandbox. I say how great it is to meet her. After 10 minutes of conversation, I probably feel the same way about her that Gideon does; she seems like a sweetheart, but I can't see that much to her, beyond the way she perches on his shoulder and makes him feel the awesome safety of warm breath on his neck. Let's face it; warm breath on your neck can take you pretty far in life.

Anthony's Hong Kong lady arrives and he introduces us all. She's not what I pictured. She looks Malaysian, and speaks English without even a hint of an accent. She's really beautiful, but also extremely tiny. I picture Anthony pouncing on her with his jock frame, and they seem a little comical together.

The porch is filling up with people I don't know. Gideon's ability to gather people around him follows wherever he goes. It's a college-type early evening gathering where everyone assumes they know everyone else but really doesn't. Eventually I go to put another shirt on over my wifebeater. I look at the shirt once in the bathroom mirror, still warm from the dryer, and remember its origin.

◆

One Saturday afternoon in late June, Anthony wanted to walk through the street fair near Astor Place. He wanted to buy a fancy lighter for his upcoming trip around the world, because the first rule of being a Traveling Man and heiress-magnet is to have an elegant way of lighting someone's cigarette for them. So me, him, and Gideon headed outside onto the baked concrete. After Anthony dropped $25 on a lighter, we found a vendor who was selling packs of A-frame tee shirts (wifebeaters). They were really cheap, but when I looked on the package, there was a small sticker that said "slightly imperfect" on the bag. We asked the merchant what that meant, but he just wanted to sell them, so he said the flaws were almost unnoticeable. We grabbed a pack and headed back to Gideon's apartment to slump in the living room, too hot to play basketball or go to the beach, too tired to write.

We saw what "slightly imperfect" meant when we opened the plastic. They were all different shapes, with a crazy variety of stitchings. We laughed at how ridiculous they looked. But when we each tried one on, they more or less fit us. Gideon's mother came home on one of her rare summer weekends in the city. There we were, striking our poses on the balcony, fervently debating global politics in our slightly imperfect wifebeaters. All his mom could say, her voice full of sarcasm, was, "Oh, isn't that nice, boys."

◆

Amelia and her boyfriend come strolling up to the porch. He's actually walking a few steps behind her tonight, looking disinterestedly away from her. I wonder if something's wrong.

Meels was my first, post-Gabe, best friend. She and I were both awkward freshman in high school together, joined by the gene-lottery curse of late-bloom and the identity-building boredom of long shared hours, partially in a basement graphic arts lab that smelled like rust and cilantro, and partially giggling through the silence together during our high school's Quaker-inspired assemblies.

Any adult with brains could've told you when we were 14 that Meels was boarding a slow-moving escalator to becoming stunningly fly, seriously gorgeous, but high school beauty politics have these nonsensical parameters, and Meels went mostly unnoticed. By the time I brought Sophie home to visit the City for Thanksgiving break of freshman year in college, Meels and I were looking at each other a little differently. At least I like to believe that. I kept her the hell away from Gideon and Anthony this summer, to say the least.

Meels spent her freshman year in Oregon, but moved back to the City to study photography. We chilled when we were home together, and she taught me about composition and light. After Sophie dissed me, I took the bus home and wandered many previously unknown neighborhoods in the outer boroughs with Meels, even Staten Island, helping her find surfaces and textures. After high school, after we both attempted the inevitable reinvention of our personalities, she developed this hushed confident intellect.

Now her voice comes at you in sudden bursts, tidy darts that make her opinions seem sharper. The sound of her voice scares me a little now, especially when she stares me down like she's about to break down everything that's gone wrong with me.

I give her a hug and kiss and she asks how Camp was. After I get over how crazy the question sounds, I say I had a great time. We catch up as I share my second forty with her.

When the porch gets too crowded, overflowing with the legions of Gideon's fanclub, we head to another party. It's a typical, overcrowded, sweaty, smelly college party, the kind that Gabe and I both despise. I try to stay as close to Meels as I can, which probably annoys her boyfriend, because he leaves almost right after we get there. A newly domesticated animal named Gideon leaves with his girlfriend pretty early on, and Anthony also goes back to his Hong Kong girl's apartment not too long after.

In our stupor, Gabe and me start a fantastic discussion in an unknown kitchen about girls. The conversation is witty and rambunctious and poetic and still somehow, kind of, sort of, respectful towards women. For once, I'm loving streamofgabe discourse. Like I said, if you can get on Gabe's wavelength, you end up loving the shit out of him, at least for as long as he'll let you. The conversation eventually comes around to Amelia. Gabe wonders aloud how Meels' boyfriend ever got with her, because he just isn't the type of kid who intrigues us, not on the surface, at least. He's studying animation, which I guess is at least creative. Gabe and I are generally super-protective of our Meels, especially now that she's officially sweated by 98.4% of hetero beings capable of erection. I say to Gabe that I don't know her boyfriend well enough to judge him, and try to change the subject.

He punches me in the arm, roaring with super-villain laughter. "YOU'RE A FAKE BUDDHIST BITCH!"" His voice is way too loud and unrestrained. "Besides, I never thought Amelia was all that great, either." He grabs someone else's used plastic cup off the counter and leaves the room to find the keg.

Meels taps me on the shoulder. She tugs me by the hand out into the backyard, pulling me beyond where any people are listening closely. For what feels like a week, she stares at me. I waver on my legs, wondering what happened to my high tolerance. My thoughts tread and then drown in the pond of malt liquor and whiskey in my fishbowl head. Meels' lips purse into a frown, but I won't realize it's even a frown until the tomorrow morning, lying remorsefully on the futon next to Gabe. Maybe it's a model's stare, or some other cheesy wish grafted into my brain. Then time goes completely glacial on me. Time doesn't exactly stop; it just gets a bad case of the hiccups in between Nows, and my mind flies off toward another moment.

[NOTE TO SELF: *There is a difference, by the way, between a memory and a moment, even if a moment technically happened in the past. The difference is that memories change and degrade, but moments don't. So what you're about to write may seem like you are reciting the memory of a memory, and therefore to anyone reading this it would just be a borrowed memory squared, but this moment exists outside time, like the Lake, returning as clearly now in 1999-Springtime Barcelona as it does when you watch Amelia stare at you in that August-1998 Random Ithaca backyard, as clearly it does when it actually happens (happens, not happened) somewhere on the Bridge over the October-1993-Forever East River, and so this one is not a memory, it is a moment, something related to but different from memory.*]

It's October 1993 on the Brooklyn Bridge Walkway, just over the halfway point where the merciful descent toward Manhattan begins. I left our high school with Amelia and Gabe and a few other friends. Everyone is surprised by the air's renewed warmth. Our backpacks are twice the size of our backs, but they feel like jet-packs instead of boulders. My brand new Digable Planets cassette lies in a silver Walkman in the outer pocket of my jet pack. I am trying to memorize the lyrics to "Where I'm From." Lower Manhattan is a towering fortress rising in front of us, moated on all sides by protective water. Last week I wrote a new poem for Grandma. She read it twice, then asked me if I knew what a patron was, saying that it's something every artist needs. Before I could answer yes she handed me a check, with no card or envelope, for $200. "Don't ever stop writing," is what the memo says.

Damien had the brilliant idea to walk to Manhattan over the Brooklyn Bridge, and then disappear down a little street in Chinatown to find this dim sum place he knows. Amelia and I think it's a great idea. After this escapade, I will ride the subway uptown to Grandma's big dark apartment, hoping the subway clerk will not scrutinize my train pass and realize I didn't get on at my school station. Grandma will then pay me the seriously nepotistic, tax-free rate of $15 per hour for my labor. I will write a few checks for her that she could just as easily write herself, and move a cabinet that does not need to be moved. Grandma will then hand me another $45, which I know she will round to $50, or probably $60 if she doesn't happen to have any tens in the apartment.

I am planning to pay for dim sum for Meels and Gabe, not because I'm generous, but just because I feel rich as hell right now. At this exact moment, I am mercilessly teasing Amelia about an older boy from the Upper East Side who she wants to unhook her bra. In her sophomore awkwardness we both know she has no chance with him. The vaults of our faces are broken open with smiles.

This moment is golden and here's the proof: The fact that Gabe and me are not at all worried about getting jumped by public school kids this afternoon, that we aren't looking around nervously for potential threats, that we have no tremors in our chests about headlock humiliations or boxcutting bullies, can only mean one thing: We are deliriously and completely happy.

◆

I am going to kiss Meels now.

I can feel the synapses starting to fire, telling my neck muscles to begin to tilt face and lips forward. I hear her voice darting through the drunk.

"Whats wrong with you Alex?"

"Nothing," I shrug and put my hands in my jean pockets. Meels stares at me hard again.

"You drink. A Lot. Really, a lot. And you used to be...so much... sweeter." *Sweeter* is an idiotic adjective. Erase it from the thesaurus; press the mute button on it. It should not be allowed to be a word in any language on any planet in the universe.

"Of course everything was better last year!" I shout at a random bush in a randomer backyard in Randomest Ithaca.

Her voice gets quiet and darting. "Not last year," Meels says. "Nobody's talking about Sophie anymore, Alex. You two were *total* assholes to each other, anyway. " She shakes her head with perfect symmetry in her negation. "I mean, I'm talking about before that."

My response wins the Retarded-Statement-of-1998-Award. "I know Meels. I know. But everything is just crazily...highly... really...temporary...right...now."

She stands there in silence for another minute and grabs my wrist again, almost like she's a doctor feeling for a pulse.

"Did Gabe say something obnoxious about me a few minutes ago?"

I can only shrug. Then, like the sister I never wanted, she tugs my hand again, but doesn't pull me toward anywhere. She just drops my palm limp at my side and walks back toward the horrible horrible awful miserable wack fake bullshit college party happening inside. She's gone by the time I can turn and walk back.

Eventually Gabe leaves to take this girl he meets home. I only see her for five seconds before he tells me they're leaving. I want to know this girl, place my stamp of approval upon her, see why *she* gets to take him. But I don't remember anything about her. I doubt Gabe does either. I stay at the house alone until the party is closed down by the cops 10 minutes later. Sitting cross-legged on the sidewalk, I put my palms together and pray drunkenly for the real world's overdue arrival. A cop asks me if I'm ok, tells me I can't sit on the sidewalk. I walk to a pizza place alone, still crowded at 2:00 am. I'm ridiculously hungry, but can only afford one slice because I'm low on cash. I listen to a drunk couple argue loudly behind me.

A cute girl comes up to me by the window and tells me I look just like a boy she knows in Philadelphia. Not in the mood, I let her have it: "Really? That's fuckin' amazing! So you see somebody who reminds you of someone you know, somebody who may or may not be really important to you. Maybe you even love the kid I supposedly remind you of. But then you decide to tell this *ridiculously* interesting fact not to the person you know, the important person, but to the person you don't know at all. But why would the person you don't know care who they look like from your wack memories, if they're never even going to meet them? In other words, what I'm trying to say is: Why do you think I care that a drunk-ass girl in a rubber-tasting pizza parlor in Random Ithaca thinks I look like some fuckface in Philly? How is that info meaningful to me in any possible way?" She looks stunned. Somehow I don't feel bad about saying it at all, and throw my oily paper plate somewhere in the vicinity of the garbage as I stumble out onto the corner.

I get lost, but eventually get back to Gideon's apartment and retrieve the key from between porch couch cushions. I collapse on the pull-out futon in the living room. Gabe comes in later, having found his way back alone somehow, and collapses on top of me in the soft mound. I don't even know how he got back to Gideon's place. He has an awful sense of direction.

"Did you fool around with that girl?" I ask groggily.

"I dunno," he answers. It's a strange response, but I'm too tired to care.

◆

In the morning my hangover rages, but Gideon drags us to the mall, because Diana is dragging him there to buy some things for their nest.

"What the fuck is a duvet?" I hear Gideon ask Anthony near the escalator. For a while, I get inspired watching Gideon and Diana roam the mall together. They're settling in. They appear almost Westchester-like. I'm happy they'll have their nest for a while, even if the whole thing is doomed. Anthony decides to see a bad romantic comedy with his Hong Kong girl, rather than spending the afternoon with us. Gabe makes fun of him, yelling "Who'd you come here to see?" as they stroll away holding hands.

While Diana is looking at potted plants across the mall, Gideon goes into a novelty store and buys a pair of g-string leopard-print panties, hiding them. We head back to their place. I try to meditate, but end up passing out on the old porch couch like a bum for hours, dreams swirling with ambient sound. When I'm half asleep on the couch, a girl I went to high school with and haven't seen since walks by. She waves, smiles wide and calls out *Alllleeex* lovingly, nostalgically. I grunt a what's up back at her and roll over.

At night we sit on the porch like old muppets, watching the college town be a college town. We compete to make the right witty comment at the right witty moment, then hold up metaphorical score cards. Amelia comes by to chill for a little while. We don't talk about last night, dancing in shared avoidance. We just talk about a sculpture show she wants to see in the City. I say I'll go with her on Friday and she nods. I tell her what time to meet for Gabe's ride to the city tomorrow, Thursday, and she leaves, probably to go fuck her boyfriend. Anthony doesn't chill with us too long either; he goes away to find his Hong Kong girl. I probably would have left, too. A few members of Gideon's Random Ithaca Fanclub join me and Gabe on the porch.

When we get drunk enough, Gideon decides it's time to put on his new leopard panties and prance. He comes out onto the porch with them on under his jeans. The girls from the apartment upstairs are all out on the other side—their side—of the porch. When Gideon's girlfriend finds out that he has the panties on, she tries to make him go inside and change, but he won't. Like morons, me and Gabe tell him to take off the jeans, as if Gideon needs the encouragement. One of the girls from the upstairs apartment says something about living in the same house as Gideon. Loud enough for him to overhear, her sentence contains the words *obnoxious* and *slutty*. That clinches it.

He unbuttons his pants and lets gravity do the rest, exposing his ass to us and his front to the girls. The problem is the panties don't cover him at all—he couldn't try them on when he bought them in the mall—and both testicles flap downwind. Little Giddy is also in full effect, shorn shaft unconfined by fabric. As a bonus, one of the girls (from Long Island, I guess by her horrified accent) has her mother visiting and helping her move in, and the mother comes out onto the porch right after Gideon drops his jeans.

He starts dancing, suddenly oblivious to everything in this galaxy but his own hips. He dances for an amazingly long stretch, as time goes glacial again. He looks like a six-year-old boy giving a lap dance to an imaginary friend, Big Bird grinding Snuffalufugus. His girlfriend is deeply humiliated, of course, screaming at him loud enough to be heard three blocks away, except he can't hear her at all. She tries to cover him with her own body somehow, anyhow, but me and Gabe are fascinated by this display, feeding off of each other like color-commentators at a Dumbass convention, spewing laughter all over the porch. Our influence can only make Gideon's stupidity glands secrete more stupid juice. All the girls and the mother are cringing. The girl from Long Island threatens to call the police.

Gideon's girlfriend starts crying hysterically and runs into the house. Ten minutes later, Gideon snaps out of his trance and goes after her.

I lift my body off the couch and walk across the porch, offering a weak apology to the mother directly. "You've got *some taste* in friends," she says to me.

"I know," I shrug. The mother heads back inside.

"What was wrong with Diana?" I ask Gabe, feigning ignorance as I come back to our side of the porch.

"I don't know," Gabe replies. "I guess she was anti-panties. I, on the other hand, was decidedly pro-panties."

"Yeah, me too," I say. "Que Vivan Las Panties!" I throw a drunken fist in the air, Che style.

The night is practically finished now, because we have to listen to Gideon and Diana fight for hours in their bedroom. The new duvet is still unopened in its plastic case on the coffee table in the living room.

Later, Gideon tells us that it took a ton of diplomacy to get Diana to stop yelling, and he really thought she was gonna break up with him, for real this time. Who gets the duvet in a divorce, anyway? But Gideon saved the situation as usual. My man can talk himself into or out of anything. I go to bed on the futon next to Gabe again, and even let myself wrap my arm around my Little Moose for comfort, when I'm sure he's already asleep.

THE BLACK MAZDA AND THE 2 TRAIN

I WAKE UP AT NOON AND GO to the bathroom to brush my teeth, realizing I haven't shaved in six days. There's some fuzzy growth in the sideburn and chin areas, but not that much. I calculate that at this rate, I will complete puberty shortly after my death, a paradox that gives me much to contemplate about the nature of time. Who's in a hurry to grow old anyway?

Meels meets us at 3:00pm by Gabe's parents' Mazda. I hug Gideon goodbye, having no idea when I'll see him again. Goodbyes don't always hit me instantly. At the moment they happen they always seem pretty inconsequential, just another few lines of dialogue. I usually space out pretty heavily during goodbyes.

Gabe drives, Anthony takes shotgun, and I sit in the back with Amelia. The ride is silent, oppressively silent, because me and Meels are afraid to talk the whole way home. The three of us are pretty drained, I guess. Too much beer and play and conversation and motion. Too little sleep, and the real world procrastinating big-time on its arrival.

For a few minutes I lay my head on Meels' shoulder to pass out, but I'm afraid I might drool on her if I fall asleep, so I sit back up. I want to talk to her about the upcoming year, about art, about nothing, about everything.

Instead I just shut my mouth and examine the ripped road map and watch us stencil ourselves on towards home. Before I know it, almost five hours later, we're on the Henry Hudson Parkway, moving down into Manhattan. We coast down the West Side Highway, the brick buildings suddenly visible over the green-gray trees, like opening the pages of a pop-up book.

"Where am I dropping you off, Amelia?" Gabe asks, his voice monotone, almost robotic.

"Oh, I can just get off anywhere uptown. I'm gonna take the cross-town bus."

"You sure?"

"Yeah, it's really no problem. Thank you so much for the ride, Gabe."

"My pleasure, Meels," he says in his patented stale voice, the closest thing to chivalry he knows.

"I'm gonna get out with her," I say. Gabe shrugs at me silently. It's nice of Gabe to drive us into the city, since he'll just turn back around and head for his parents' place in Ossining anyway. I wonder if it's hard for him. The City has this unbelievable nostalgic force, this City-kid bat-signal you will always cry out for if you grew up here. I wonder how much Gabe feels it. He always makes me stop with him and talk to his Super when we roll by his old building on Hudson Street.

He absentmindedly mentions that he'll probably come into the City sometime next week, but I remind him I'm leaving the morning after tomorrow. For a moment I get mad at him for not remembering my schedule, but then I let it go.

"We'll definitely call you tomorrow, Alex Bardo," Anthony says heroically. They're planning to drive to South Carolina for a few days, and I wonder if Anthony will have another love affair with some dixie heiress down there. The black Mazda creeps away, and the backs of Gabe and Anthony's heads get smaller behind pin-striped glass.

Gabe won't leave for London until the middle of September and Anthony will head to Dublin a week after that, so at least they'll have each other, for a while.

◆

I'm struggling to start a good conversation on the corner when Amelia speaks.

"That ride was so depressing," she says. "I wanted to talk to you but everyone was so...silent."

"Yeah, I know," I shrug.

"You still want to go to the show tomorrow?" she asks.

"Yeah, definitely."

"Are you sure? Don't you have to pack?"

"I can pack in like 20 minutes, Meels," I say.

"Oh right, I forgot. You're a *boy*," she laughs a little. "Call me when you're up."

I give her a kiss on the cheek and watch her flee to the Broadway bus stop, her own large duffel bag strapped over her shoulder. Daylight is fading, and the street level is crowded with shadows. Up above, over the tenth floors of buildings, the lowering sun turns brick and glass to gold and brass.

Sometimes when people have their backs to you, they look even more beautiful, unless that's just how memory messes with moments. I watch Meels all the way down the block, which drawls slightly uphill, so she ascends. I stand as still as I possibly can, transfixed by the peacefulness of her gait. I must look like an idiot on the corner of West End Ave. At any moment Meels could turn her head and see me watching her, but in that case she'd be looking at me too, so I'm safe. I want to reach out my arms all the way to her as she goes, stretch out like Plastic Man, to grab her and wrap my arms around and around her at least 19 times, to memorize her. But I have no super powers, and no time machine to go back three minutes either. Of course, I could just be courageous and sprint across the street like a maniac and catch up to her.

[NOTE TO SELF: *That note that you wrote earlier, the one about inventing a time machine, that's not a good idea. Everything you said about Jorge and Buddha is all right, but you shouldn't invent a time machine. That's not what courageous people do. Courageous people hate time machines. Courageous people also don't stay up for four days in a Barcelona hostel writing nostalgically, sipping liters of Cruzcampo they don't even want to drink in celebration of arbitrary solo 21st birthdays, just because the Cruzcampo liter sorta kinda reminds them of a few good memories of Olde English forties on a Washington Square balcony. Courageous people definitely don't invent time machines to go back to ask Jorge Luis Borges or Buddha unanswerable questions about love. And for that matter, courageous people don't invent time machines to go forward a few years just to see if Alex and Gabe will even know each other anymore. Courageous people have no need for time machines. Courageous people invent* Now-Machines.]

◆

I fish a quarter out of my duffel and slot it in the Bell Atlantic pay phone on the corner of 96th and Broadway. I tap digits I know not by sight, but by touch.

"Huhlo?" Dad's voice reaches over the scratch of his cordless phone. He sounds all blissed out. Instantly, I know exactly where his body is in space, can see his Martin acoustic guitar, a rose-print on the leather strap, lying on his lap. I can etch-a-sketch the hunch of his body on the couch, the sunset somewhere back behind Soho and the Hudson River and New Jersey streaming in the window, turning the graying hair on his neck to silver-white. I tell him I need to see him, that I'll be downtown in half-hour or so. He says, "Of course," the way he always does. There are two Negra Modelos and one half lime in the fridge, he says.

I get on the subway at 96th and Broadway, swiping my Metrocard through the turnstile and seeing that it still has $12 left on it. That means eight more trips there's no chance I'll take before I leave. Maybe I can give Meels my Metrocard when I see her tomorrow, but she only buys the old tokens, defiant against the coming automation of the 21st Century. Hurtling underground on the 2 train, somewhere between 59th and 50th streets, I pull out my heavy key chain and examine it. I already have 16 keys (including the useless Victorian skeleton key Sophie gave me as a 19th birthday present a year and a half ago, and the keys to Grandma's country house). Sixteen keys is too many. I look across the subway car and see a homeless man sprawled out across three seats. It occurs to me that there's objectively a right number of keys to have on your chain, and if you have too few or too many you're basically homeless, either way.

As I leave the train at Times Square to switch to the N/R line, I hear a gruff voice. It's my Inner Gabe. "That thought you just had," Inner Gabe says, "that thought about having too many damn keys and somehow claiming that you're homeless…that particular thought, my brother from another mother, is just *retardedly postcolonial.*"

ALEX BARDO'S WANNABE POETRY
Vol. 1

A Wary Invitation to my Future Child
for my Mother

And you that shall cross from shore to shore years hence,
are more to me, and more in my meditations, than you might suppose.

Walt Whitman, "Crossing Brooklyn Ferry"

1. The Disclaimer

Let me just say I'm not expecting you for a while
Except by tragedy of bubble-burst latex
You won't come wailing anytime soon.
So if all goes according to the Plan
according to Which nothing ever goes
you should be slowly wrapping things up in your last life right
     now
taking long walks and talking nonsense to strangers and
     drooling a little bit
trying to untie mental knots
making temporary peace with those apparent contradictions
getting affairs in order
just so that others may grieve what I welcome.
Maybe you're a satin-clad Goddess riding a long-tusked
     elephant
or maybe you just got world peace declared on the Planet
     Zolton
or maybe you're that eccentric horseshoe crab misunderstood
     by all the other horseshoe crabs whose genius as a
     horseshoe crab will only be recognized long after a lonely
     death in a lonely horseshoe shell.
I hope you're not a consultant.

2. The Fine Print

Aggression still tantalizes us
(I'm sorry)

Obsession's like a bungee cord
(I'm sorry)

Delusion emits a steady hum
(I'm sorry)

Your father's a crazy buddhist
(I'm sorry)

Kids don't get to make any decisions
(I'm sorry)

Parents argue over money and then slam doors shut
(I'm sorry)

Adults make three lists: one short list called "Friends," a longer
list called "Enemies," and a really long list called "Who Cares?"
(I'm sorry)

Old people scream "I wish I could have done more!" which
nobody understands because their words are slurred by strokes
and tears.
(I'm sorry)

If two people look each other in the eye it's usually by accident
(I'm sorry)

When people dance they get embarrassed
(I'm sorry)

When people speak they feel self-conscious
(I'm sorry)

When people smile they look guilty
(I'm sorry)

We have this little thing called propaganda
(I'm sorry)

We have this big thing called poverty
(I'm sorry)

We have these huge things called armies
(I'm sorry)

There's no escape from your own mind—believe me I already
tried Everything
(I'm really really sorry)

You will become what you hate—it's inevitable
The only way I've found to deal with this is to expand the scope
of what you love
(I'm not sorry)

3. *The Invitation*

Where you are now, do they have cartoons?
Where you are now, do they sip maté?
Where you are now, do they have paintings where the oil leaves
        a 3D trail across the canvas?
Where you are now, did they reinvent the wheel yet?
Where you are now, are there kaleidoscopic cities?
Where you are now, are your fingers mesmerized by the gray

texture of the mortar which holds a brick wall together?

Where you are now, do they have Bob Dylan?

Where you are now, does your body come with two of
everything, just in case?

Where you are now, do genitals interlock *so* perfectly, and then
separate like defective velcro?

Where you are now, do all your teachers sneak up into the
crawl-space between thoughts and haunt you?

Where you are now, do friends sit crosslegged in a circle playing
conga drums until a half-hour past a cloudy dawn at which
point they all rise together and cook Eggs Overtired with
salsa, and between yawns and mouthfuls scream without
apology the most arrogant statement ever made: "let's save
the world!"?

4. PostScript

At the bottom of a cardboard pile in a just-sold house in Arkansas
is a pristine photograph of a grandfather who dies of a fourth
heart attack just as his grandson reaches the ripe old age of
negative 1 (Earth years). He holds a baby girl and he looks just
like me. Or I should say that I look just like him, that is, if we
want to be polite and pretend that a circle is a line.

Bushwick, 2002

Smiley Face

That isn't the recipe for a wink
All that semicolon, end parentheses
With the occasional squiggly line in between
Anthropomorphizing towards nose

Whoever invented that keyboard combination
Must've fancied himself a savior
Marveling at the removal of Time and
...Space...from the act of flirtation

Time and space are a package deal
They'll eventually rebel against eviction
Returning offline to teach devout coquettes
The truth about dancing eyelids:

Getting a real wink, you want to run away
What subject ever volunteers for objectification?
Giving a wink, you want to run even faster
Who knew that Being requires audience participation?

The wink itself feels nothing but mischief
Sliding ninja-like under barbed wire and
Through that porous fence which quarantines
Self///////////////////from///////////////////////////Other

Humanity's first avatar was the drum
Shorthand for the skin over sternum over ♥Beat
There was something so tender in that representation.
Maybe it was the skin.

Oh, emo boys and girls, emoting, motionless,
Prostrate before pixels, wired in clouds

That shadow behind the L.E.D. screen
Is the silhouette of a cheek

And your emoticons won't save you
From a smile.

Austin, TX 2011

Movie Ticket

My lady buys me a $12 gift.
I reciprocate with red Twizzlers and
32 ounces of Mugs Root Beer
on my priceless Visa Card
(a poem about a movie should
match its product placement).
Our seats recline almost as far
as we'd like them to.
We hold hands as
the black sidekick dies
in the second scene.
He does not protest.
After 30 minutes,
a supermodel makes a cameo.
She does not smile.
At the 60-minute mark,
the villain's motives are clarified.
They are not complex.
In Minute 95, the protagonist, a true heroine,
gives up everything.
She relinquishes:
Fame and Fortune and Beauty
in exchange for:
Truth and Love and Wisdom.
She performs this ritual sacrifice
surrounding us with SurroundSound,
surrendering Self
so that the Producers and I
never have to.

Union Square, 2009

Dear Don

Dear Mr. Rumsfeld,
That thing
you said
about the two kinds

of ignorance:
the things we
know we don't know,
and the things we

don't know
we don't know —
That was brilliant
utterly brilliant.

Now I will
always consider
you one of
my teachers.

Sincerely, me.

Toronto 2004

Urban Planning

1. The Ancestors

They plant their banner before they know its meaning
Bodies emerging at low tide
Leaving bare footprints in the spongy soil
Impaling the dirt with a sharp flagpole
A prick to the scalp of this fresh ground
Not knowing what will come of their proclamations
Because they haven't even imagined the symbolism
Knowing that they must proclaim something

to ensure the impossibility of a clean slate.

2. The Survivors

They spend nights huddled under rough quilts
Sewn from the scraps of discarded beliefs
They survive bleakest winters, hibernating from anxiety's blizzards
Dreaming of demons left somewhere back on the other side
Of that great gulf their parents crossed
That ocean which swallows memory, but excretes impulse
And everyone forgets so easily that Fear knows how to swim
a steady dog-paddle

to ensure the impossibility of a clean slate.

3. The Settlers

In Springtime they clear a space for themselves on new terrain,
defining the space and themselves as they go.
Not knowing where their definitions will lead,

because the settlers haven't developed a vocabulary.
But convincing themselves that they have to define something

defining space with

Blacksmiths and horseshoes and little houses built from the masonry of another world's stone and steeples and fiery impromptu sermons on wooden crates and work ethics and beaver pelts and the trading stations of materialism's furry warmth and taverns and corn whiskey and festivals and drooling lovemaking and parched starvations and nearby colonial cannonball wars and 24-dollar-plague-buckshot-genocides

and seasons generations lifetimes

to ensure the impossibility of a clean slate.

4. The Citizens

Now the flag flies high in the Square
the symbolism remains unclear and language can only square
    dance around it.
Yet there is much more to build, much room to grow.
Growth will solve all their problems, even ones they haven't
    grown into yet.

Growing space with

Cobblestone pavements and factories and thick black furnaces and materialism's industrial mushroom cloud and waves of immigrant concepts rolling in through the harbor's gaping mouth and puppet governments and ferriswheel bureaucracies and the spires of cathedrals and the domes of temples and steam engines and monumental architects and lightless tenements built from the brick and mortar of hollowed expectations and townhouses and long bannered parades and groping lovemaking and tubercular lonelinesses and far-away colonial artillery wars and not-so-far-away cotton-clad-sugar-cane-ball-and-chain-dominations and seasons generations lifetimes

to ensure the impossibility of a clean slate.

5. The Consumers

The flag has been updated, logo rebranded
It heaves and flaps, sleek in the wind above the metropolis
historians no longer pursue its meaning.
Instead the consumers adorn the space of the city,
That's what reflex tells them to do

adorning space with

Smooth cement avenues and boutique hotels and caffeine-opium dens and organic cellophane-marts and the mounting debit card digits of materialism's new paperless trail and cages and academies and water treatment plants and housing projects constructed from the concrete of a timid mind and Goldman-skyscrapers erected from the glitter of that same mind and the true Terror of duality's unsolved mystery and fantasies scrawled across buildings and thought-bubble graffiti and dogwalkers marching in unison with virtual poodles and homeless junkies slumped against cosmo junkies on benches and monumental billboards showing larger-than-life-faces-of-fear and ok-computer-cupid lovemaking and wireless seclusions and far away colonial night-goggle wars and not so far away pill-popping-unstoppable-sitcom-depressions and seasons generations lifetimes accelerating accelerating accelerating
to ensure the IMpossibility of a clean slate.

6. The Commuters

In a little park in a corner of the Metropolis
There is a plaque next to a statue beneath a flagpole.
The plaque has finally defined the symbolism and set their
    language to bronze:
"The Settlers set forth to create this City Upon A Hill,
They did so for their posterity and for their posterity's posterity
To erase the deep scars of History
And to ensure the Possibility of a Clean Slate."
A mediocre joker, an unpublished prophet, a vandal with a thick
    sharpee
has inserted the letters **IM** in front.
You should visit this park on your commute.
Look it up in your traveler's guide.
Between laughter and remembrance,
An appreciation takes root.

pushing downward
into the gum-stained pavement
Once called Earth
Reaching upward
into the longing smog
Still called Sky

In between the two,
In the logoless Gap®
where past doesn't yet
bind future
aggression will fall
to peaces.

Aw, Nuts
for Ian Koebner

This
This Mantra
This Mantra used
This Mantra used to
This Mantra used to come
This Mantra used to come in
This Mantra used to come in handy

In
In moments
In moments like
In moments like these.

Aw
Aw, Nuts

The
The World
The World is
The World is falling
The World is falling apart.

Aw
Aw, Nuts

Falling
Falling Apart,
Falling apart yet
Falling apart yet again
Falling apart yet again, my

Falling apart yet again, my friend.

Aw
Aw, Nuts.

That's
That's what
That's what the
That's what the World
That's what the World does.

It
It falls
It falls apart.

Awwwwwwwwwwwwww,
Nnnnnuuuuuuuuuuuuuuuuuutttttsssssssss!!!!!!!!!!!!

Middletown, CT 2005

The Problem With Spooning (Or, The Opposite of Regret)

Sometime around 5am
This bottom arm may need amputation
Buried alive under her shoulder girdle,
left for dead on the darker side of numb.
Maybe if we drilled a hole
down through mattress and frame
And let the thing dangle
Everything would work itself out in the
(No-really-morning-breath-is-cute,
Let's-go-out-for-breakfast-and-sit-on-the-same-side-of-the-
     table,
Let's-dive-onto-sidewalks-performing-pdas-at-every-corner
Let's-be-*those*-people-*that*-couple)
Restedly-ever-after morning.

Around 4am
This nose, buried in itchy tangles
 will have a shampoo flashback
(Possessed of the power to instantly propel
The sniffer back through
dead milky-ways of intimacy,
Shampoo flashbacks are the most confusing trauma
Known to Nose.)
This nose has been around the olfactory block
And can testify at last that
there are fewer brands of shampoo
than there are heads of hair.

Sometime around 3am
this skin will wax pseudo-scientific
And wonder if two organic masses each set to roughly
98.6 degrees Fahrenheit

Can in their proximity generate 197.2 degree heat
Or if this inferno of limbs is only imaginary
(Where are the physicists when you actually need one,
The supposed know-it-alls regarding
the attraction and repulsion of forms
Those masters of thermodynamics and friction
Where are they now
When not the cosmos, but the next date
is at stake?)

Around 2am
This brain will obsess over anthropologies
And think back to its
Great-great-great-great-grandparents
Scattered throughout mongrel Europe
Wondering how their slumber might be studied
(Just answer one simple question, mind:
Did our ancestors care for each other, and spoon accordingly?
"I really don't know."
Then just answer three complicated questions, brain:
Is affection anything more than the perfection of comfort?
Is lineage just the restful angle of skull in crook of armpit?
Is nuclear family just the reliability of good nights' sleep?)
This brain will take mercy at last upon the past
Even if mercy is just a synonym for
exhaustion.

Around 1am
This chest will recoil from its counterpart
Within this torso throbs a cupcake
Lathered with a thick frosting
of rust.
When this chest burrows into her back,
it begins to worry that the rust will smear her shoulders

that it's actually possible
to corrode another's ribs,
That there's serious danger of
Communicating disease.
(Chests are generally advised to consider
Some form of protection against the mutual infection of
All that scar tissue, which keeps masquerading
as Maturity)

At this very moment , as Bodies fall asleep, their deed well done
A sudden optimist is born
(The best optimists are just *like* that
—Sudden—
They have no context for history's atrocities
And shrug off the 100% likelihood of coming dystopias)
The top arm, that liberated,
enlightened arm
Look at that thing go!
Draping itself like a matador's cape
Across her breast, tugging gently
That top arm is without a doubt
all crushed out. In love, maybe even?
(Easy, now!)
The only practice left
Is one sole act of restraint
Please, Oh Body, the top arm *begs:*
Don't roll over
And play dead.

Los Angeles, 2011

Offering

I thought
I was generous
until you asked
for the thing
I didn't want
to give away.

Listening

I thought
I was a good
listener.
Wait…
wait…
what'd
you just say?

Practicing

I thought
I was
a great meditator
until there was
no one there
to watch me.

Preaching

I thought
you were
nodding in agreement
until I saw
those headphones
in your ears.

Origins

The Origin of Ignorance

As babies
We had crystals to see with, no eyelids.
Pupils did not shrink from that margarine light.
Soon, bored by our burps, we beat ourselves senseless.
Sobbing in cribs with the fragments of prisms.
We've plotted vengeance against blindness
Daily, since then.

The Origin of Love

As toddlers
We waddled to the park with our parents.
Our Faces abstracted by Grass-Mustard-Chocolate,
We ran in huge spirals and made crazy sounds.
We unleashed a cry that shook the bars of the jungle gym
When mommy motioned toward the twilight that had
Just been the sun.

The Origin of War

As children
We played god with a huge pile of Legos
But you stomped on the castle that I built from scratch
I used scrap paper to make origami battalions.
My most deranged teddy bear was unopposed to torture.
The playmobile walls of your fortress are still
Splattered with blood.

The Origin of Lust

As a teen
You sat on a couch looking wounded
Recalling a script which invented a Player
I reached for your jeans and then asked how you felt
And now I'll be stalking you across time, space,
and bodies, just because you shrugged and pulled your
Leg back an inch.

The Origin of Pride

Too early
We were told to list our credentials.
I typed up my deeds and statistics to match.
A whole CV of fantasies, based loosely on fiction
The bold arial font was a twelve-point transgression.
How high can you get off glue from an envelope,
Stamping it "mine."

The Origin of Ideas

In college
We were taught only one foreign language
We studied the Language of Assumptions as much as we could
Becoming fluent, we Assumed
We could explain our Assumptions
Meanwhile, our professors, The Assumptions, became
Fluent in Us.

The Origin of Origins

It's not right
To say that the sperm makes the egg

And it's also not true
To think the egg births the sperm
In a 5-act daydream, they each storyboard "other"
Without aching for romance, tadpoles will never
Begin to swim

A PostPostModern Definition of Egolessness
for the inner nihilist

Listen, moron. I'm only gonna explain this to you one more time. I'm sick of you pretending to understand. I'm sick of your unexamined privilege. I'm sick of the fact that you think you've already understood your privilege. I'm sick of the fact that you think you're a victim of privilege. I'm definitely sick of the humongous vocabulary you keep reinventing, just so no one can understand you. All the art you've masterminded comes from fear. You plagiarized other plagiarists. Your words and your actions have never even met each other before, and now they fumble through introductions like two nervous people on a bad blind date.

You think what they're trying to teach you is you don't exist? Where'd you get that, *Spirituality for Dummies*? Why don't you take your overpriced statue of Avalokiteshvara back to the trendy Tibetan store it came from. Get your money back and buy some dvd porn and ecstasy; at least that'd be honest.

Really, you don't exist? Does that explanation explain anything to you?

Does that explain what your mother was feeling as she gave up her art for you?
Or the way a pen can dry up on you at the exact moment the word arrives? The inexplicable fact that both apathy and kindness are contagious? Does it explain the presence of cantaloupes and smart bombs? What gravity does to giant red planets and tiny rubber balls? Does nonexistence explain why you try so hard to explain everything?
Does it explain my exhaustion, knowing I've already explained

all this a million times, and will have to explain it again tomorrow, and the next day and the day after that, too?

This life is not a black hole.

It's a house of cards floating in space
The cards are so perfectly arranged
Push even one and the whole structure changes
Touch the walls and you'll see the cards are liquid
heaving into each other
glistening, shedding, sweating salty little dewdrops of
    consciousness
The atmosphere buzzes birth and hums death
Whispering: "S-U-C-H-N-E-S-S"
Nothing so beautiful could be a construct
I definitely don't blame you for trying to narrow it all down to
    catchwords
But for once just look at the house!
It hovers in naked space
And you, the moron, always try to anchor it down to something
Good luck with that, Sisyphus
The anchor weighs a ton

You want to know what they mean by egolessness?
They mean that actually you do exist
And no one else is responsible for this house.

Colorado, 2006

The Last Thing

Someone ate the last cookie but left
The last sip of soy milk in the carton.

One last piece of the jigsaw
went missing from the box.

The last comic book I ever read is now in storage,
next to a baseball card that's probably worth something.

Your very last hairclip was found under the bed-frame,
only three years after you moved out.

The last thing the guru ever said to me
was "hello."

The last song
was performed without encore.

The last wizard departed Earth long ago,
convinced we were taking truth too literally.

During the last ice age
people complained less about the weather.

During the last eon
the galaxy went to preschool.

The last analog moment
is now available for download.

The last moment of silence
is live-blogged as we speak.

That last nervous breakdown resulted in
a more spiritual form of ambivalence

We made our last wish at 11:11. It came true,
making everyone nervous

Before apathy took over,
our last fixation was Hope.

Before compassion set in,
our last realization was Loneliness.

That last thought
will not last.

The last thing a fish sees
is the water.

The last thing a person sees
is the mind.

Providence, RI, 2011

ETHAN NICHTERN is the author of *One City: A Declaration of Interdependence* and a founding member of the Sacred Slam poetry performance series. He writes and blogs for a variety of websites. When not writing, he is a Shastri, senior teacher in the Shambhala Buddhist tradition. At 33, he is the youngest empowered senior teacher in the global Shambhala community. He is also the founder of the nonprofit organization the Interdependence Project. He is based in New York City. This is his first volume of fiction and poetry.

Many thanks to my parents, to my teachers—especially those who have taught the dharma of life and the dharma of writing, to the lifelong parade of close friends and heartbreaks, especially those who shaped me when my path was taking shape—you do make experience truly worth recording, to my awesome editor Nadxieli Nieto Hall, to my genius publicist Lisa Weinert, to Jerry Kolber who gave this book its title via g-chat, to Doug Einar Olsen who brought the Emoticon to visual life, to my students who share the primordial poetry of thoughts and emoti(c)ons, and finally to Claire Nichtern—in my dream you are reclining in your chair, discussing things that really matter, comfortable and awake.